It was difficult for Josey to believe her good fortune. She felt only a little sadness when she thought of Ellen gone to La Crosse. They had parted as friends and exchanged e-mails.

Josey had never had a lover who wanted her so much. In the months since she and Lauren began making love, Lauren's insistent passion never failed to arouse her own.

"Come on, take those horsey clothes off." Lauren started unbuttoning Josey's flannel shirt.

They were in too much of a hurry to bother with completely undressing. Lying in a tangle of limbs, panting in the aftermath, Josey knew slower, more satisfying lovemaking would follow.

Josey felt completed for the first time in her life. Never was she lonely anymore . . .

Visit

Bella Books

at

BellaBooks.com

or call our toll-free number

1-800-729-4992

Woman in the Mirror

Jackie Calhoun

Bella
BOOKS

2004

Bella Books, Inc.
P.O. Box 10543
Tallahassee, FL 32302

Printed in the United States of America on acid-free paper
First Edition

Editor: Anna Chinappi
Cover designer: Michelle L. Corby

ISBN 1-931513-78-3

This is a work of fiction,
dedicated to those who have endured breast cancer.

Acknowledging my new editor, Anna Chinappi,
the persuasiveness of Linda Hill,
my first reader, Joan Hendry,
and my live-in reader, Diane Mandler.

Spring

I

Josey

With the bathroom door safely locked behind her, Josephine Duprey stared at her reflection. The surgeon had taken the bandages off earlier in the afternoon and this was the first time she'd found the nerve to study his work. The raw scar crossed with vertical strips of tape climbed in an obscene smile across the space her left breast had once filled, then fell in a frown, rose again, and ended in a downturn under her arm. The surrounding flesh was crudely gathered in. The tube that had drained blood from the wound into a plastic cup was gone, and fluids not yet absorbed by her body moved under the pale skin. The cancer had been in the ducts. Intraductal carcinoma in situ. Rather common, she'd been told. Very small in her case. Stage zero.

Apparently if you had to have breast cancer, this was the type to have. However, the word had inspired enough fear that she'd gone along with the suggested mastectomy. The biopsies had shown the invasive cells hadn't spread beyond the calcium deposits that had been biopsied in an earlier surgical procedure. She could have kept the breast and undergone radiation or chemo and taken tamoxifen. This way, though, she knew she was cancer-free and able to skip the treatment she could ill afford.

After swearing her good friend and business partner to silence, she'd asked Mary Durban to take her to the surgeries and bring her home. There'd been so little pain, first with the surgical procedure and then with the mastectomy itself, that she'd sent Mary on her way the mornings after, shooing her out the door with the words:

"I'll call if I need anything. You look after the shop. Sell some of my paintings. That's what will really help me."

Financially this had been a disaster. With an uncertain income and a twenty-five-hundred-dollar deductible health insurance policy with eighty/twenty coverage, she'd be stuck with huge bills, even though both surgeries had been outpatient. She'd bargained on not getting seriously ill when choosing a major medical policy, and lost.

She'd done her crying between surgeries when the reality had sunk in, sobbing her grief into the pillow. It was something she'd never thought would happen to her. Breast cancer ran in families, or so she thought, and as far as she knew, hers had none of it.

When the oncological surgeon recommended a mastectomy, Josey had already suggested that Ellen Lignofsky move in with her. They'd spent so many nights together. However, she shrank from sharing the news with Ellen, of going ahead with their plans to live together. So she hadn't told her about the cancer, had instead said that her niece was coming to live with her and she wanted to get acquainted with the girl before she progressed on to anything else.

Which was pure bullshit. She'd been annoyed when her sister Liz called to tell her that Annie had been suspended from the university and lost her scholarship. The girl had been arrested for underage drinking at a party where someone had died from alcohol poisoning. Would Josey take her niece in? Charles, Liz's worthless husband who

4

was not Annie's real father, had said the girl couldn't return home. She was twenty and on her own.

"Not even if she finds a job?" she'd asked. Charles had married Liz when she was pregnant with Annie, and Liz had been sucking up to him ever since as if he'd done her a big favor.

"It would be better if she lived with you. She can't afford an apartment. She's been staying with friends. It's just for a while, Josey. Till she gets her head together."

Exasperated, she'd said, "It's your house, too. You could put your foot down for once."

"I've got three other kids. When they're gone, so am I."

"*Sure*, Liz. You and the kids could come live with me right now. You could find work in the Clover Hospital or the clinic." Would she like that? No privacy, her chance lost of picking up with Ellen where she'd left off.

Liz ignored her suggestion. "I don't know what's going on with Annie. She's never been in trouble before."

She knew she should tell Liz, who was her twin, about the cancer, but the words stuck in her throat. To talk about it was to acknowledge it, something she cringed from doing.

Not only had the operations plunged her into debt, but knowing she had cancer had thrown her into a state of anxiety. Perhaps she would feel better after the plastic surgeon scheduled reconstructive surgery. When she looked like nothing had happened, at least with her clothes on, maybe she'd find some reassurance. Now she awakened every few hours during the night.

Almost manic with undirected energy, she'd lost her ability to concentrate. The few paintings she'd worked on during the two months between surgeries she considered garbage.

The girl was due to arrive today. She pulled a large T-shirt over her head, hoping it would hide the empty space, and decided to wait for the kid in the garden.

Jerking a handful of grass out of the ground, she shook the sand off the roots impatiently. Working in the garden once soothed her.

Now the monotony of it, the time to think drove her wild. Buddy, his eyes fixed on her, lay at the end of the row of lettuce she was weeding.

Smiling a little at his devotion, she said, "You could lie in the shade, you know. I'm not going to run away."

The dog's tail beat the ground at the sound of her voice. Last winter she'd found him on the side of the road where he'd been hit by a car and left to die in a snowbank. She preferred to think the driver hadn't seen him or thought he'd been killed outright. Approaching the injured dog with trepidation, she'd slid a blanket under him when he licked her hand and put him in the back of her '90 Ford Escort wagon. The vet bill had cost several hundred dollars, which she could ill afford, but she'd paid it and taken him home after a week.

When she spied the old Jeep Wrangler coming down the driveway in a cloud of sand, she straightened and shielded her eyes with a hand. "Come on, fella, let's go say hello to Annie."

The medium-sized dog, with a curly brown coat of hair that pointed to some poodle or maybe cocker heritage, was already racing toward the vehicle. His misfortune had not made him mean or afraid of people, and he seldom barked. As far as she was concerned, he was the perfect companion.

The girl stepped out of the Jeep and squatted to greet the dog. She looked up as Josey approached, and Josey took her in with her eyes. She hadn't seen any of her sister's kids since she and Liz had buried their parents. Annie had been about ten years old then.

Her niece's gray eyes studied her in return. The girl stopped stroking Buddy and ran long fingers through her own hair, a nearly black cap of thick waves. "Nice dog," she said, standing up. She was alarmingly thin, which her baggy shorts and T-shirt emphasized. "Are you my aunt?"

"If you're Annie Spitz, I am. You look like your mom." Of course, that meant she looked like Josey too. She glanced at the flawless sky. "It's hot." Reaching into the back seat of the open Jeep, she grabbed one of the smaller suitcases. The doctor had said not to lift anything heavy for a couple of weeks. "Let's go inside."

Striding ahead of the girl toward the house, she saw it as her niece must with the white paint peeling off the old structure. She had rented a pressure washer weeks ago and blown off the loose flakes. It was ready to paint, but she had neither the money nor the time, and now she was saddled with a lot of medical debt.

Going in the side door near the rear of the house, she passed through the mud room into the kitchen, which she'd never updated in all these years. The old stove, the rounded refrigerator, the porcelain sink still functioned well enough for her. The few cupboards crafted long ago from pine boards were darkened with time. Worn yellow linoleum covered the countertops and floor. The curtained door on the back wall hid the opening to the pantry, where she stacked the shelves with canned and dry goods.

It was the house where she and Liz had grown up, which she had bought from her parents' estate using most of her half of the life insurance for the down payment. At the time, she'd found herself unable to part with the family homestead and its furnishings.

Setting the suitcase down, she turned to catch the girl staring at her unsold paintings, their vivid colors set off by the white walls, and saw them anew herself. "Would you like some iced tea?"

Annie turned toward her, her gray eyes huge in her narrow face. "Mom said you were an artist. Are these yours?"

"Yep." She forced a smile. She had so many paintings that she rotated them between the house and the shop. Taking a bottle of iced tea out of the fridge, she filled two glasses. "I'm prolific if nothing else."

"They're wonderful," Annie said.

"Thanks," she replied, thinking if that were so they'd have sold. "Sit down and tell me what's going on." She believed in bringing everything out in the open, which was maybe why she'd given Ellen a gentle push out of her life. She'd have had to talk about the mastectomy and how she felt about it otherwise.

Annie slid into a chair and stroked Buddy, who thumped down next to her looking for a handout. "Didn't Mom tell you the university kicked me out and Dad said I couldn't come home?" Her face flushed, and she hunched her narrow shoulders as if to make herself smaller.

"Yes. I thought I should hear your side if there is one." She sat, too.

"I was at a party where someone died," Annie mumbled, her eyes on the dog. She took a deep breath and plunged on, "Mom said if I could stay with you it would be better. As soon as I can, I'll find a place of my own."

Josey reminded herself that it was her sister she had a grievance with, not this girl. "No need for that. There's room to spare here. Have you given up on college?"

Annie threw Josey a look of despair. "I've lost the scholarship. It wasn't enough anyway. I worked part time and Mom busted her butt to come up with the rest of the money. I don't know if college is right for me anyway."

"It's hard to get anywhere without a degree." She was a good one to preach, since she didn't have one herself. "I thought your mom would bring you."

"She had to work, so she told me to take the Jeep. Dad's going to be pissed when he finds out, but he only uses it to haul stuff he won't put in his car. It doesn't even have a top. He says it runs on luck. I don't care as long as it runs." She gave a shrug.

Since Josey was unable to talk about Charles with any dispassion—he did that to her—she clamped her lips tight. When they'd downed their iced tea, she slapped the tabletop. Annie jumped. "Sorry. Want to see your room?" She was halfway to her feet before the girl scrambled to hers.

Annie gestured at the walls as they left the kitchen. "I used to like to draw. I wanted to take art, but I'd never be able to paint like this."

"How do you know if you don't try? And why didn't you?"

"Dad said he wasn't going to buy the materials so that I could dabble. But if he saw what you've done, maybe he would have."

8

She snorted her answer, knowing whatever else Charles had said would not flatter her. Besides, her living came from painting portraits, not from the likes of the pictures on the walls. They were her passion. She headed up the stairs to the second floor, the steps creaking under her weight.

The room at the top of the stairs was furnished sparingly. It had once been hers and, as then, it held a double bed with iron posts, a bedstand with a small lamp, and a maple dresser with a knob missing on all four drawers. A curtain covered a small closet, and two tall, double-hung windows looked out on the backyard and the woods beyond. Even though Josey had hung some of her brightest paintings on the white walls and scattered a few rag rugs across the plank floor, the effect appeared Spartan.

"My room's at the end of the hall here. There's a bathroom between the two, which we'll have to share." Josey's bedroom had been her parents' and resembled this one in size and furnishings. However, it faced both south and west, where sun and moon flooded it with light and the prevailing winds cooled it during the warm seasons. "This is an old house," she said almost apologetically. "Cold in the winter, warm in the summer."

Annie looked pleased, though. "It's huge compared to my room at home, which I always had to share with Jeanne." Her younger sister. "The one at the university was tiny, too."

"I'm glad you like it. I'll leave you here to unpack while I go finish the weeding. Then I have to run into town and check up on a few things. You can come if you like, or stay if you don't."

Back in the garden she cut the lettuce and spinach that sprouted bright green against the sandy soil and stuffed them in a paper bag. Where once she would have sat on the porch and read till Annie was unpacked, now she found herself unable to sit or concentrate on anything for long.

Since she had let Ellen Lignofsky slip from her life, Josey had avoided the house, spending most of her time at the Pottery and Art Mill where she worked with Mary Durban. When Mary was making pottery, Josey tended the shop, and when Josey was painting, Mary took care of customers. It worked out well. She considered Mary her best friend and closest confidante.

Buddy flopped in the sand at the end of the row and followed her with his eyes. Before long Annie came walking through the thin grass, circumventing the patches of blooming daisies that Josey had carefully mowed around. She cut the grass maybe three times a season, leaving the bunches of wildflowers to grow unchecked.

The girl stood uncertainly at the edge of the garden until the dog got to his feet and, tail wagging, trotted over to her. She knelt on one knee to pat him. "Can I help?"

"I'm ready to go if you are. Or would you rather stay here?"

"I'll go with you."

Josey straightened, stretching out the kink in her back. "Let's take the greens inside and I'll wash up."

The Mill, which had actually functioned as such at one time, stood next to the dam that created the Clover Mill Pond. The waters of the Cottonwood River ran through it. Fed by springs and small creeks, the trout stream wound for miles through fields and woods, growing ever larger and more sluggish, finally emptying into one of the flowages in the next county south. Here at the mill the rushing water gathered and thickened before surging over the cement barrier. Darting just out of the water's reach, cedar waxwings and swallows snatched insects in midair.

Josey parked her rusting Escort next to the building. She never tired of the small, noisy waterfall or the mill pond that attracted so much wildlife. "Come on. I'll introduce you to Mary Durban, my partner in art."

Nor did she tire of the building, which smelled to her of sweet grain and dust when she first entered it. Motes danced in the light shafting through the windows. The interior was always cool on the hottest days, even without air conditioning. Something to do with the high ceilings and the cold water of the trout stream that made up the mill pond. Mary Durban had bought the place nine years ago when it had been on the market for more than a year and after Josey agreed to join her in operating it. Together Mary had thought they'd make a go of it. And after a fashion, they had.

Mary's pottery adorned every surface. Bowls, plates, and other useful items, artfully formed and beautifully glazed. Josey's paintings lined the walls. She had so many that most were in the back room along with Mary's unsold pottery, yet the two of them continued to produce their art apace. When the cancer was detected, the passion that had bordered on obsession for Josey fell dormant.

"Hello, the mill," Josey called, pulling the large wood door to behind her. It groaned the last few inches before latching.

"Hello, the back room," Mary replied.

Their voices echoed off ceiling and walls. Ears flattened, the dog raced off to find Mary who crooned to him, "Sweet little Buddy."

"I could make off with the till." Josey poked her head through the inner door to the studio, leaving Annie to walk around the shop.

The wood planks protested the girl's slight weight. She paused before each piece of art, gazing at the paintings and pottery in silence.

"I hear when somebody comes in. The creaking door tells all and what it doesn't, the floor gives away." Mary got up from her wheel, her hands gray with clay.

She smiled and Josey thought, as she had many times before, that it was good that Mary Durban was a heterosexual woman because she was also a dark-haired, dark-eyed beauty with a quick wit and an enviable talent. Next to Liz, Annie's mother, Josey loved Mary best.

"Ellen was in earlier. She left a book for you. Said she thought you'd enjoy it."

Josey's heart lurched a little, just enough to let her know that Ellen still dwelled there. Time would take care of that, just as it had done with Bev five years earlier. When Bev first left, Josey had thought the pain would never go away. Now it was almost as if Bev had never been.

She wondered why Ellen seemed to have no wish to leave town. As head librarian of the Clover Public Library, she could have looked elsewhere easily enough. These weren't Ellen's stomping grounds, after all. They were Josey's.

"Did you bring your niece with you?" Mary asked, washing her hands at the sink in the small bathroom. "Is that who I hear, or do we have a customer?"

"My niece. Come meet her."

Mary wiped her hands on a ragged towel and followed Josey into the shop. "You're a reflection of your aunt. Only younger, of course," she said to Annie.

"No, she's the image of her mother, my twin," Josey corrected.

"There are beautiful things here," Annie stammered, throwing a nervous glance at Josey. "I had no idea."

"Why would you?" Josey asked with lofted eyebrows.

"It's so nice. You know? The building, the pond, the falls, the paintings and pottery." The words rushed out. Annie's face grew pinker with each one.

The girl meant it, Josey could tell, so she forgave what she considered gushing. "Yeah, well . . ."

"Thanks," Mary said simply. Mary never downplayed compliments. She graciously accepted them. "You're here to stay a while, I hear."

"Until I find a job and a place of my own." The girl smiled shyly, looking nervously from Mary to Josey and back again.

Josey had passed on to Mary the story Liz had told her. They exchanged a glance and Mary winked. "Did I ever tell you, Josey, that I got thrown out of college, when I turned my room into a studio and skipped every class but those with art in them?"

Her mouth slightly open in surprise, Annie stared at Mary.

"Yes," Josey said bluntly, "but underage drinking is in a whole different category."

"I did plenty of that too and so did you, Josey. We just didn't get caught."

The evident discomfort of the girl stopped Josey short of saying someone had died at the party where Annie was caught drinking.

"So, what are you two doing here? I thought you were taking the day off, Josey."

"I was, I am. I'm just showing Annie around." Josey picked up the book on the counter and turned it over in her hands. It was a fishing mystery written by a Wisconsin woman.

"An entertaining read, Ellen said. She also said you haven't been stopping by the library. That's why she took the liberty of bringing this book to you." Mary gave Josey a hard stare. "How can you stay away from the library?"

"I haven't finished reading all those books your sister gave you and you gave me."

"Ellen misses sharing books with you," Mary said.

"She said that?" Josey looked at her niece, wondering what she made of this conversation.

"Yeah, she did. Now you two go on and enjoy the rest of the day. Tomorrow you can work, Josey. And Annie, I expect to see a whole lot of you." Mary bent over to pat the dog, who licked her hand. "I love you, too, Buddy."

The phone rang when they sat down at the pine table for supper that night. Josey had broiled a couple of small steaks, nuked two potatoes, and put together a salad out of the greens she had picked in the garden.

"That'll probably be Mom," Annie said as Josey got up to answer the old wall phone with the rotary dial.

"Hi, Liz. Yep, she got here all right. I thought you'd bring her, though."

"I had to work. Didn't she tell you?" Liz said.

"Yes." Josey eyed her niece as Annie took a few bites of the salad. "We're just eating supper. Looks to me like she could use some weight."

"Well she never was one for putting on pounds. Too hyper. Did she tell you she'd paint your house for her keep?"

"No," Josey said. "I can't afford paint anyway."

"I'll pay for it, and I'll come visit as soon as I can. I promise. Now let me talk to Annie. Charles will be home soon."

She held the phone out to her niece. "You're right; it's your mom."

At the table Josey cut her steak into small pieces while listening to Annie's side of the conversation.

"I'm okay. What did he say about the Jeep?" The girl wrapped her body up in the phone cord. "I need something to drive. This place is really out in the boonies." She unwound herself slowly and stood still for a moment. "I would have told her. I just hadn't gotten around to it. It's a big house."

"Well?" Josey asked when the girl hung up, slid into her chair, and began to eat. "Do you get to keep the Jeep?" She'd thought the vehicle looked like an accident waiting to happen, but so did the Escort.

"For now. Have you got a ladder? The check for the paint's in the mail. I may as well get started."

"I'll show you where everything is after supper. You can charge what you need at the hardware store in Clover." She must have mentioned the need for a paint job to Liz. She vaguely recalled talking to her sister when she was pressure washing the house.

II
Annie

Annie walked around all sides of the three-story farmhouse, attic included, trying to decide where to start. She wouldn't get very far with less than a gallon of primer, which was what Josey had scrounged up the night before. Maybe it would be best to drive into town and get some more.

Josey had left Buddy behind that morning, for company she'd said. Buddy sat in the driveway, looking in the direction where he'd last glimpsed the Escort. Annie felt sorry for him.

The Jeep's torn, black seat burned her butt when she slid behind the wheel as it must have the dog's because he hopped from foot to foot next to her, testing before sitting. Annie grabbed the ancient beach towel she'd stuffed on the floor in back and spread it across both seats.

On the road the hot wind tore at her hair. Glancing at the dog, she smiled at the sight of his ears floating in the breeze, his eyes nearly shut, a grin on his panting face. Moisture dripped off his tongue.

"You dogs know how to live," she said, running a hand over Buddy's shoulders. "In the moment." And she vowed to try, instead of dredging up all the things she wanted to forget, like that guy convulsing on the floor at the party. The one who'd died at the hospital later. She shuddered, remembering.

Why she'd crashed that party and gotten bombed out of her head and then didn't have the sense to get out of the house before the police arrived, she'd never know. It had turned into the biggest mistake she'd made in a long string of errors that took over the last year of her life. Stupid, stupid, stupid.

She hadn't even cared when Charles, her stepdad, said she couldn't move back home. He wasn't really her dad anyway. Why call him Dad? He never liked her. She never liked him. In truth, she didn't think he liked his own daughters any better.

Slowing down when she reached Main Street, she looked for Menken Hardware and saw the *Ace* sign hanging over the sidewalk. Pulling up to the high curb in front of the store, she stepped out of the Jeep and grabbed the gallon of leftover paint off the floor of the back seat.

"You stay here, Buddy," she said, worrying a little about leaving him sitting in the open car with the sun beating down. The doors on the Wrangler sagged and she lifted hers a little before shutting it. A small chunk of rust fell off the lower door panel.

A bell jangled over the door as she entered. Fans whirred overhead from the high ceilings, and the floor boards squeaked underfoot as she made her way down a narrow aisle toward the counter. The aisle continued on to where a door opened. A pickup was backed up to the double doors of a storage building across the unpaved alley.

A girl about Annie's age—she still thought of herself as a girl—

stood behind the counter paging through a magazine. She looked up and gave Annie a friendly smile. "Can I help you?"

"I need some primer like this. Do you have it?" Annie asked, plunking the leftover gallon on the counter.

"Sure. How many gallons do you want?"

"Two for starters. My aunt, Josey Duprey, has a charge account here?" It came out as a question.

"Yeah, I know her, but I don't think I've ever seen you before." The girl pushed a ladder over to the shelves behind the counter and climbed up a couple of steps, took down two gallons, then teetered for a moment while Annie held her breath. When she regained her balance and got off the ladder, she put the paint on the shakers.

"I'm Deanne Spitz," Annie said, giving her full name.

"I'm Molly. I work for my dad here summers. I don't know where you come from, but it's pretty dull around here if you don't know where to go." Molly leaned across the counter confidingly.

"I come from Milwaukee," Annie said, taking in Molly's long curling lashes and large chocolate colored eyes, her thick brown hair tucked behind tiny ears, the dimples when she smiled. She compared Molly's skin to her own, thinking maybe she could get a tan like that working outside this summer. "Your last name is Menken?"

Molly nodded. "In grade school the kids called me M&M."

"Yeah? They called me DeeDee the chickadee. The boys preferred Spitzer, after which they'd spit of course. Everyone else calls me Annie." She was warming up to Molly fast. "Where do you go when it's dull?" She wanted to be there too.

Molly shot a glance at the open back door and lowered her voice. "There are certain bars where we all hang out." She stopped talking when a man appeared in the alley doorway, blocking the light. It was impossible to see anything but his shape.

"Hello." He nodded but came no farther inside. "I'm going to deliver these doors, Molly, if you don't need me."

"Okay, Dad. I'll be fine," Molly said.

Her father climbed into the truck and drove away. The shakers stopped vibrating and silence took over, except for the radio. Molly unfastened the gallon containers and put them on the counter along with a stir paddle.

"There," she said. "Sure you don't want more? That's a big house."

"This'll get me started. I'll be back."

Molly stuffed her hands in the back pockets of her jeans and grinned. "I don't envy you. Come on out to the Little Fox on Diamond Lake Tuesday night. About nine o'clock. I'll introduce you to some people."

"Maybe I will," she said, blocking out a vision of the guy jerking on the carpet, vomit leaking out of his mouth. She'd sworn off beer after that. "Thanks."

"Don't break a leg," Molly called as Annie left, passing someone coming in on her way out.

Setting the cans on the floor by the back seat, she grabbed the hot door handle and jerked the door open. "Poor thing," she said to the panting dog. "We better stop and get you a drink of water at the Mill." It was just down the street at the edge of town.

She parked next to her aunt's Escort. Buddy hopped out of the Jeep and ran down to the pooling water at the base of the falls. Grabbing at branches, she slid down a steep, narrow pathway to where the dog already stood on a flat rock, lapping water.

The cool spray dampened her face and she leaned into it, then bent to feel the foaming icy cold water on her fingers. A red-eared turtle, its neck all the way out, watched them from a log that jutted into the stream on the other side. The turtle plopped into the water as she and the dog scurried up the path to the parking lot.

Buddy trotted toward the front porch. She followed slowly, unsure of her welcome. When a woman opened the door on her way out, the dog wagged his tail and slipped inside.

"Hey, Buddy. Where did you come from?" the woman asked and nearly bumped into Annie. "Hi." Her bright blue eyes honed in on Annie with interest. "I'm Ellen Lignofsky." She stuck out a hand.

18

Annie took it with a bemused smile. "Annie Spitz."

Ellen showed her a beautiful smile, set off by one lone dimple. "Josey's niece. Are you a reader like your aunt?"

"Yes," Annie said. She always had been. Her stepdad had carped about her reading when she should have been doing something useful. She'd even written some short stories, aspiring to be an artist in some form.

"Well, then come see me at the library. If we don't have a book you want, we can get it." Ellen's blond curls fell to the nape of her neck and shone in the sun. She was slim and as tall as Annie.

"Great."

"Now I have to get back to work." Ellen started toward the road on foot.

"Do you need a ride?" Annie asked.

"No thanks. I'll walk."

There was nothing to do but go inside after the dog. Three women were wandering around the interior, exclaiming about the art. Josey looked up from behind the small central counter and spotted her niece.

"I figured Buddy didn't walk to town on his own."

"We came in to get more paint and it was so hot he needed a drink. But then he rushed on in here, so I came to get him." She was surprised to find herself blushing.

"You can leave Buddy here," her aunt said. "The customers like him."

Annie turned toward the door. "Okay."

She drove back to the farmhouse at a leisurely pace, taking in the wildflowers in the fields, the oak and pine woods. She was in no hurry to start painting.

At the house she walked around all sides again, then began on the southern exposure, the one facing the garage and outbuildings. It was what her aunt would see first. Stirring the paint in the old can until it was smooth, she slathered it on the bare spots. It splattered on the roses that grew next to the foundation, the thorns of which were tearing at her bare legs. The sun beat down out of a clear sky and she felt the rays penetrating the sunblock she'd smeared on herself. Even the sand warmed her feet in her tennis shoes.

At noon she went inside for a drink of water and a peanut butter sandwich. The silence was getting to her. The birds that had been proclaiming their territory with song had quieted in the heat of the day and there was no traffic, no people, not even any insects. She was used to noise. It had accompanied her around the city.

It was lonely here, she decided as she sat at the kitchen table, trying to concentrate on a book she found in a living room bookcase. She couldn't believe she came here without taking any reading material. She'd sensed her mother's hurry to get her out of the house before Charles came home.

Everyone who had been arrested at that party had been suspended from the university. If she hadn't been in such shock, if her mother hadn't been called, she might have stayed in the city and found work. But she doubted she could afford to live in Madison on her own. So here she was in lieu of a better place.

Long after she devoured the sandwich, she put down the book. While she quickly became fascinated with the family portrayed in its pages, in her mind, they were nuts. Even her family wasn't as crazy as this one. The kids hid from their alcoholic father. The mother had kicked him out, but it looked like she was going to take in a con man who even the kids could see through.

Outside, the sun blazed summer hot. She moved around the corner to the west side, the back of the house. The sun was heading in that direction, but it wasn't there yet. She had finished the leftover can of paint and opened a fresh one, stirred it briefly, then began brushing over the bare spots. It would take a long time to make her way around the house. Weeks and weeks, she figured. Maybe she'd be out of here before it was done.

With plenty of time to think, she found herself avoiding thought. At school she'd begun to skip classes that bored her, like sociology and economics. She either fell asleep over a chapter or failed to recall a single sentence from the text in either course. In fact, she had difficulty staying awake. Period. It was like she was on a downhill slide that ended at that disastrous party. She'd only gone because Sue Kingston, her friend across the hall who slept her days away, invited her.

Annie had at first studied hard, ignoring the partying that went on. She was lucky to be at the university, she knew. If she hadn't gotten the scholarship, Charles would have insisted she get a full-time job. He'd never gone to college. He sold cars. It was her mother who stood behind Annie, who insisted she get as many years of higher education as possible. Now it looked like three was the limit.

Just when she was getting used to the silence, she heard the sound of a vehicle coming down the road, turning into the sandy driveway, arriving in a cloud of dust. She turned and squinted in its direction as it pulled up next to her Jeep. There was a sign on the door, but she couldn't read it.

"Hi." A girl got out of the F150 truck and walked through the tall grass toward her. A ballcap covered her hair.

With dripping brush in hand, Annie stared until she recognized Molly. "Hi. What brings you here?" Annie's gaze moved over Molly's long legs, slender, muscular, tan, and continued up her slim, athletic body to her eyes.

Molly pushed her hands into the pockets of her shorts and shrugged. "I was delivering some stuff for my dad not far from here and thought I'd stop. I needed a break from the store."

"Want to come in for iced tea or something?" There wasn't anything else to drink except water. She'd looked for Coke or Pepsi. She put the brush in a plastic bag and covered the paint with the lid.

"Sure. I've never seen the inside of this house."

They walked into the kitchen through the mud room, past the boots and hanging coats, and Molly stopped in her tracks as Annie had when she first saw the paintings. "She's good, isn't she?"

"Yeah, I think so." Annie got the pitcher of iced tea out of the fridge and poured a couple of glasses. She sat down at the table. "Feels good to get out of the sun."

21

"It's the sand," Molly said, pulling out a chair. "It reflects the heat. You ought to see your face. It's fried."

"I can feel it." Annie put the cool glass against her cheek and shivered.

"You should wear a hat." Molly touched the brim of hers, above which read *Ace Is the Place*.

"I don't have one."

Molly placed the ballcap on Annie's head and snugged it down. "Now you do."

She laughed. "I can't take your hat."

"Sure you can. Free advertising for the hardware store. Dad would approve."

"Okay. I'll wear it. Thanks."

"I should go. Dad'll be wondering where I am. I'm expecting to see you at the Gray Fox on Diamond Lake tomorrow night."

Annie said, "I'll try to make it."

When Molly drove away, Annie reopened the lid of the paint can and began slathering it on again. The hushed heat made her sleepy, and whatever thoughts she had slipped away without taking hold.

III
Josey

Josey was ebullient after selling one of her watercolors and several of Mary's pottery pieces. They were lucky to sell a few hundred dollars worth of art in a week during the tourist season. Off season, weeks passed without a sale.

On the phone that afternoon she agreed to another job and, after closing, planned to take a look at the horse she was supposed to paint. Portraiture was a form of painting, and if not the kind she wanted to be known for, it afforded her practice and money.

No subject was beneath her. She'd painted dogs, cats, sheep, cows, goats, and horses with their owners and without. It was the time taken from her other painting to do these portraits that she once objected to. She often had to remind herself that her portraits allowed her to continue her passion.

Mary emerged from the back room just before five. She tossed her dark hair and lightly poked Josey in the ribs with an elbow as Josey took the checks and cash out of the register. "A good day, huh?"

"Too bad it's not a typical day," Josey said, handing the money to Mary, who had a safe at home.

"You took on another portrait, didn't you?" Mary had inherited money from her grandfather, not a huge amount but enough to live on exclusive of her work.

When they locked the door behind them, still chattering about the day's sales, they were surprised to find Roy Schroeder sitting on one of the porch chairs, smoking. He leaned over to fondle Buddy's ears. "You can always count on a dog to be glad to see you," he said.

"How's it going, Roy?" Josey walked quickly past, not wanting to hear Mary yell at him.

"Good, Jose. You sold some of those great paintings?"

"One, but now I have to go see about making some real money."

"Where this time?" he asked as Buddy ran after Josey.

"Bud and Brenda Lovelace's."

"Horses make nobler pictures than their cloven-hoofed barn-mates, don't you think?"

"I guess. Whatever pays." She waved and hurried toward her car, but she wasn't quite out of earshot.

"What the hell are you doing here?" Mary asked.

"Can't we work something out, babe?" he inquired before Josey got into her car.

The rest of the exchange she could guess at. Mary would tell him there was nothing to work on, to leave her alone. She was still smarting from finding out the hard way that Roy was inclined towards men.

As Josey backed out the Escort, Mary marched toward her car and Roy strode along beside her, pleading for some compromise. Watching them in their impossible situation saddened Josey. They were both beautiful people. Roy, rough and rugged-looking, tall and muscular with a grace of movement not given to most men. His curly hair was receding, leaving him with an impressive forehead. His deeply set grayish-green eyes were shaded by thick curling lashes.

She ached for them, because there was no solution to the love they felt for each other. They had to get on with their own agendas. Mary was trying. Roy was in denial. He seemed to think he could have it both ways.

Though she'd left the windows open, the temperature inside the Escort had to be in the nineties. The air conditioning no longer worked, so the only way to stir up a breeze was to drive. Buddy stuck his head out the passenger window, sides heaving, the drool off his tongue splattering the back window. Outside of town, she stepped on the gas, but the hot air pouring in the windows offered little relief. Way too hot for May, she thought.

The stable was on County E. The sign read *Lovelace Quarter Horses* and showed the head of a horse. She turned into the paved driveway and drove a hundred feet or so past board fences, backed by high tensile wire. She wished she had the money that had been spent in fencing this farm. Parking under a large oak, she left the dog in the car and made her way to the stable.

In the aisle, highlighted by sun flowing through skylights and side lights, a tall, elegant horse stood in the cross-ties. It swung its long head in Josey's direction as the people standing around the animal turned at her approach.

Fans whirred in the aisleway and stalls, giving the illusion of cooling. A sheen of sweat layered the horse's coat and the Lovelaces' faces. She felt drenched in her own.

"Hi," she called as she neared. "Pretty horse." A safe assumption. Why would they want a portrait of an ordinary one?

She knew Brenda Lovelace, but she had only seen Bud once or twice when he was in town with his wife. Their son, John, she'd glimpsed on occasion at the feed mill, picking up grain when she was buying seed and plants for the garden.

Bud smiled tolerantly at her ignorance of horseflesh. "This guy is a superior halter horse and a superior western pleasure horse. His babies are winning futurities."

"I'm impressed," Josey said with no clue as to what a futurity was.

"Thanks for coming out." Brenda gave a short laugh. "Don't mind Bud. He's a little proud. It's as if he thinks he produced Monty himself."

"I would be too." She told the white lie with a smile. "Thanks for the chance to paint him. Can you bring him outside, so I can take some photos?"

John unfastened the cross-ties, replaced the plain leather halter with one encrusted with silver, and hooked a leather lead to it. The stallion ambled out of the barn obediently.

Outside, she heard barking and glanced uneasily down the driveway. A doberman was circling her Escort. Alarmed, she said, "My dog's in the car, and I had to leave the windows open. I didn't want to go home first."

Bud whistled and the large black dog galloped toward them, coming first to Josey. She froze as he sniffed at her crotch. A low warning rumbled in his throat.

"Put him in a stall, Bud," Brenda said.

"He won't hurt anybody," Bud protested.

"I'll do it," John said, handing the lead to his father and going back in the barn with the dog.

"Dobermans get a bad rap," Bud grumbled, as the horse craned its long neck in the direction John had taken.

"Can you pose Monty the way you want him in the portrait. I'll take some photos and run them by you later."

"Front-view photos make a horse look narrow. It's best to photograph from the side," Bud said.

"She does this for a living, Bud," Brenda pointed out.

"That's okay. I'm open to ideas." Josey backed up a little and put the camera to her eye.

John returned to take the lead from his father. The horse welcomed him by knocking him off balance with his nose. John grinned and scratched behind the animal's ears.

Josey photographed the stallion from all angles and with different backgrounds. In front of the stable, before a fence with a field of grass behind it, and finally beside a pond in back of the stable. If she was lucky, she'd sell them the photos, too.

When she got home, she was surprised at how much Annie had done in one day. The south side of the house, as far up as was reachable from the ground, had been patched with white primer. Going into the kitchen, she set her camera on the table and headed up the stairs to change.

She was forced to wear huge shirts to hide the imbalance caused by the mastectomy. She could have worn the bra the hospital had provided, which she'd probably paid for, but she had gone braless for years now and had thrown it in a drawer just in case. It was damned inconvenient to have this happen when it was so hot out.

Putting on shorts and a T-shirt, she went downstairs. It was close to seven. Annie must be starving. Buddy had followed Josey inside, looking for dinner, and she filled his dish for him.

The night before, she'd taken leftover lasagna out of the freezer. She now put it in the microwave and started tearing up the lettuce and spinach that were lying on the counter. With that done, she went in search of Annie and found her on the porch, engrossed in a book.

"I heard you come in. I just wanted to finish this chapter. I picked some lettuce and spinach."

"I saw. I should have told you I'd be late. Did you eat anything?"

"I had another peanut butter and jam sandwich mid-afternoon." Annie put the paperback down and Josey read the title. *Songs in Ordinary Times*.

"What do you think of it?"

"These people are weird."

"Dysfunctional is the word."

"My mom would never kick my stepdad out, even if he was a drunk. He probably wouldn't go anyway. But she's not stupid enough to be conned by that guy in the book."

"Probably not."

"You don't like Charles, do you?"

"How'd you guess?" Josey turned the light on in the kitchen. Clouds had piled up, blocking the sun.

"I don't like him either," Annie said. "He's not my real dad, you know. I don't want to call him Dad anymore."

She studied her niece. "Don't then, and yes, I know he's not your real father." The girl's gray eyes glowed out of her sunburned face like orbs of ash. "You got a lot of painting done. Did they give you the hat at the hardware store?"

"Yep," Annie said, pulling on the brim. "I'm advertising."

"You must not have had it on all day." Josey took the lasagna out of the microwave and put it on the table. "Do you know anything about horses?"

"No, why?"

"I have to paint one. I've done a couple of 4-H horses before, but this is a super horse. That's where I was, at the stable taking pictures."

Annie looked bemused. "I didn't know you painted animals."

"People and animals. Portraits. That's what pays the bills, not these pictures on the walls." She tasted the lasagna and realized how hungry she was. "I'd paint a chicken if someone paid me to do it."

"Why'd Mom marry him?" The kid's eyes had never left Josey's face.

"You'll have to ask her."

"It was because she was pregnant with me, wasn't it?"

Josey put her fork down. "Look. Your mother loves you. She was in a bind. We all make mistakes, but she didn't have to marry him. There were other choices."

"I'm never going to marry anybody," the girl said, taking another piece of lasagna.

"You're kind of young to say that."

"I'm like you."

Josey choked on a drink of water. "What does that mean?"

"You know." If possible, Annie's face darkened further in a blush. She hid her surprise with a frown. Was it hereditary? Did Liz suspect her daughter was a lesbian? If so, she hadn't let on. Sighing, she imagined the words Charles had used to tell Annie her aunt was gay. She let it go without comment. She had no one now. She was celibate.

When she drove out the next morning, the air was thick with the smell of coming rain and already hot despite low clouds that covered the sun. She left Buddy home with Annie, who was covering her open Jeep, using bungee cords to fasten the blue tarp in place.

Josey developed her own black and white prints, but not color, so she mailed the film at the post office. Mary's Taurus wagon was parked outside the Mill when she pulled in next to it. Josey found her in the studio.

"So what happened with Roy last night?" she asked, looking out the dusty windows at the mill pond. The still water reflected the gray clouds.

Mary glanced up from glazing a plate, her eyes as black as the swirls she'd painted on a background of bright blue. "I told him to get lost. I just wish he'd move away so that I could get over him."

"His business is here." Roy owned and operated Schroeder Log Homes.

Mary shot her a dark look. "Every time I see him I want him. I don't know what to do with it. You should understand. Only you had no good reason to give up Ellen."

"Hey, let's not start the day like this. Okay? I made my choice. You made yours. Maybe they're both bad. You could co-exist with Roy."

"While he runs around with the guys. Are you nuts?"

"Find some other man. That shouldn't be hard. You're gorgeous." Then she held her breath for a moment while the silence grew. She felt Mary looking at her, but she refused to meet her eyes. Instead, she watched a breeze skitter across the pond's surface.

Mary sighed. "If it were only that easy. Anyway I don't want another man. I just want him to go away, so I don't miss him so much. Does that make any sense?"

"It does to me." She hadn't really painted anything worthwhile since the surgery and felt no need to start now. "You go ahead and work. I'll tend the shop."

"How did the portrait thing go yesterday?"

"Bud Lovelace is an arrogant son of a bitch, but his wife and son are nice. I think it'll be all right. Painting a horse beats doing a cow or a sheep. There's something noble about a horse." She laughed. "And this is a super horse."

"Why don't you do a real painting? You haven't worked on anything for a couple of months, do you realize that?"

"I will when I'm ready. Anyway, I've got so many real paintings, as you call them, that I probably should give it a break."

She figured it would all be resolved when the mastectomy stopped seeming such an outrage. Then she'd paint again. She went into the shop and opened the door to the public.

It began to drizzle as she stood on the porch. She thought she saw Ellen on the edge of town, pausing to open an umbrella. "Damn," she muttered as her heart fluttered against her ribs. There was no escaping the woman.

She backed herself inside and closed the door.

IV
Annie

She sat at the kitchen table, scribbling in a tablet while the rain fell outside. These were the days of computers, yet she'd never owned one. The book had inspired her to write about her own family, barely fictionalized.

My first memory of the man I called Dad so many years was of him sitting in his chair in front of the TV, yelling for Mom to take me away. I was about three and had toddled over to him to touch his leg. It was like my hand burned him.

I remember hesitating before fearfully reaching toward him, knowing somehow that he wouldn't like it. I wanted to feel the texture of his pajama bottoms. They looked so soft.

He jumped, making me jump, and I began to cry when he yelled for my mother. Both of us were hollering when she rushed into the room and picked me up.

"What did she do, Charles?" she asked.

"She touched me," he said as if I were disgusting.

I still remember the shame and the hurt.

Did she? Vaguely. The touch that brought his howl of anger, she recalled. Her own bawling response and her sense that something about her was repellent, that also. What her mother and Charles said to each other, she guessed at. What could she say? He didn't like her. She wasn't his child, but Jeanne, Holly, and Lisa were. Them he only ignored. Did she care? She had done everything she could think of to please him while growing up. Excelled in school and sports, worked on the high school yearbook, sung in the choir, played clarinet in the band. She'd never once heard a word of encouragement or approval from him.

However, the indifference he'd shown her was nothing compared to his contempt for Josey. No, the kids couldn't go to their aunt's, he'd said, when their mother planned a weekend visit. Nor was Josey welcome in their house.

"I'm not letting that woman pervert my kids. What kind of a mother are you anyways, Liz? You go see her, but don't bring any of her ways back here."

During her preteen years she was fascinated by this aunt who drew such scorn from Charles. She looked up *pervert* in the dictionary, coming up with definitions of "corrupt" and "one given to sexual perversion," which captured her interest even more. What was sexual perversion? There was no one to ask except her mother and she didn't dare. Charles might get wind of it.

She looked outside the windows at the rain, coming down unabated. The dog lay at her feet, heaving an occasional sigh. She returned to the tablet.

When my mother brought Jeanne home from the hospital, I stared at her red, wrinkled face for a long time, trying to figure out why Mom wanted her, especially when Dad was lamenting about another girl. Couldn't Mom produce a boy?

Why was a boy better than a girl? I asked Mom when he was gone.

A man always wants a son, just like a woman always wants a daughter, Mom said.

You've got me, Mama, I replied. You don't need Jeanne.

I need you both.

When she finally realized that Charles didn't want her to excel at anything, that he wanted her to fail instead, she couldn't let herself fall short lest she live up to his expectations. And she hadn't, until that fatal party, which gave Charles a reason to tell Mom she couldn't return home.

Had it ever been home? She frowned at the rain falling and decided that wherever her mom was would always be home. She glanced at the clock. It was late afternoon, and she closed the notebook and carried it to the porch, where she curled up in a chair and read the book that had prompted her to write.

At five o'clock the rain stopped, and she dumped the water out of the tarp covering the Jeep. The wet grass dampened her legs and soaked her tennis shoes. She hadn't forgotten that this was the night Molly would be at the Gray Fox on Diamond Lake. She looked up Diamond Lake on the county map that was pinned on the wall near the kitchen door. She'd have to drive over and check the place out at least.

Going out to the garden, she shook the greens off before piling them on the grass. As she did so, the clouds moved away from the sun so that its warmth spread over the yard.

When she told Josey at supper that she was going out, Josey looked at her with interest. "To the Gray Fox?"

She nodded. "How did you know?"

"That's where we always went."

Annie tried to envision a young Josey, and failed. "Molly said a bunch of her friends were meeting there tonight."

"Russ's daughter? She give you the ballcap?"

"Yep." This was a little like being questioned by her mom at home.

"You'll be driving and drinking."

"I had my last drink at that frat party."

Josey gave a short nod. "Watch out for deer. They start moving around at dusk."

Driving to the Gray Fox on dark roads, the only lights a million stars in a blue-black sky, she nearly hit her first deer. The animal jumped out of the ditch and bounded across the road, first appearing in her headlights not more than two feet in front of the Jeep. She caught sight of twin fawns frozen in fear on the sandy berm. Had they followed their mother, she would have surely hit them.

She was still shaking when she got to Diamond Lake and spied the bar tucked into a curve on the south side of the lake. Lights flooded the parking lot, holding back the night. People stepped in and out of their glare.

The night was humid and warm as if it hadn't rained at all. She got out of the Jeep and stood uncertainly on the sandy lot, working up enough courage to go inside.

Inside, the smell of beer and cigarette smoke enveloped her. The juke box blared, vying with the televisions above the bar for attention. Squinting, she scanned the place for Molly.

"Hey there, pretty girl. Looking for someone?"

The guy, grinning at her with two beers in hand, had red hair curling around his ears and freckles marching across his pug nose. He was tall and thin with pale blue eyes under eyebrows lofted in question.

She returned the smile. "Molly Menken."

"Want a beer?" he asked, holding a foaming glass out to her.

She gave up her resolve. One drink wouldn't hurt and it might allay the nervousness she felt. "Thanks."

"I'm John. And you?"

The cold beer slid down her throat, soothing her. "Annie," she said. "I'm staying with my aunt."

"And your aunt is?" He cocked his head.

"Josey Duprey."

"She's going to make our horse immortal. Are you an artist, too?" She stopped looking for Molly. "Sort of. Not a painter, though. More of a writer. You own the super horse?"

John laughed. "My dad owns the super horse. I just train him and show him."

"Yeah? What do you train him to do?" Her interest was piqued.

"To stand at halter and be a pleasure to ride. He's won enough quarter horse points that people bring their mares to him to breed. Come out and see him. He's a prince among stallions."

"Maybe I will," she said. Her one contact with horses had been unfortunate. She'd gone with Sue to a friend's house near the university and let herself be talked into riding one of their horses. When Sue and her friend cantered, Annie's horse bolted for the barn. Sure she was about to die, she had embarrassed herself with her screaming. Horses held no allure for her.

"Hey, Annie."

She looked for the voice and caught sight of Molly threading her way through the crowd toward her. She raised her hand in greeting.

"Hi, Lovie," Molly said to John when she reached them. "Have you been taking good care of her?"

"My nickname," John explained. "The kids couldn't resist. It was Lovie or Lacie."

Annie looked puzzled.

"His name is John Lovelace," Molly said. "Sorry, John. I should know better after being called M&M all those years."

"Well, you look good enough to eat," John remarked. "You two want another beer. I'm buying."

"One's enough," Annie said, remembering her broken pledge.

"I do," Molly said. "Come on, Annie. I'll show you around."

As Molly propelled Annie through the crowd, she occasionally brushed Annie's arm with her body. Goosebumps radiated up and down Annie's skin. Molly called out people's names as she went and Annie nodded and smiled, knowing she'd never be able to match these names with faces. At the bar, a handsome young man drew Molly aside and whispered in her ear. Molly laughed and Annie felt a stab of jealousy.

"Want to see the lake?" John asked, handing the promised beer to Molly.

"Sure," Annie said, as the other young man put his arm around Molly.

John took her hand and gently pulled her toward the open patio doors that led to a wood deck. Outside, Annie took a deep breath to clear her lungs and smelled the lake, a combination of weeds and water and fish.

"I've got some good stuff. Want to share?" John led her to a swing set on the sand beyond the deck.

"I thought we were going to see the lake," she said.

"We can go for a swim," he suggested as they approached the beach.

The lake glittered under the stars. Lights from cottage windows lit its perimeter. "I don't have a suit on." She kicked off her sandals and waded into water cooler than the air.

"I don't either. We've got shorts on, though." He stepped out of his loafers and walked in. "You can swim, can't you?"

Swimming was one sport she hadn't participated in. She'd never mastered the strokes. Instead, she'd learned to keep her head above the surface using a cross between a dog paddle and the breast stroke.

They swam toward a raft floating within the buoyed swimming area. Climbing up the ladder after John, she sat next to him, her feet in the water along with his.

"This beats the bar scene, doesn't it?" he asked.

"Yes," she admitted, wishing it was Molly sitting next to her. She looked at the heavens reflected in the black lake. "In the city, you don't see the sky at night. There's so much other light."

"I know. I go to UW—Madison."

"I was there, too," she said.

"Yeah? What's your major?"

"Journalism." Although she hadn't been able to envision herself as a real reporter, writing was her only consuming interest other than reading a good book. "And yours?"

"Pre-vet." He leaned on his hands, idly kicking his feet in the water.

"That makes sense with the horses and all," she said.

"Then I can pretty much choose where I want to live."

"Here?"

He turned his head toward her. "Yeah. You probably think I'm nuts to want to live in this backwater."

"Hey, who's out there?"

Annie's heart gave a little leap. Molly was not alone, though. Whoever was standing with her was male, tall with broad shoulders.

"Water's warm," John called.

"I'm coming out." A few minutes later, Molly climbed the ladder alone.

It felt to Josey like a small triumph, Molly leaving the guy on the beach.

"What's with you two?" she asked, sitting between them.

"We're communing with nature," John replied.

"You don't have anything to smoke?" she inquired.

"It's on shore. Should I swim in and get it?"

"Yeah. Why don't you?" Molly lay back on the raft. "We'll wait, won't we, Annie? And don't invite the guy on the beach, if he's still there." She tugged at Annie's arm till she lay next to her, staring at the stars.

At that moment, Annie didn't need marijuana or beer to make her any happier than she was.

When she drove in the driveway and made her way to the porch, she wondered why the dog was frolicking around her feet.

She jumped when her aunt said, "You're all wet. Isn't the water kind of cold?"

"Not really." Annie stood dripping at the bottom of the steps. "Around here they arrest kids for drinking and driving."

"I had one beer." Annie saw the glowing ash and smelled the burning tobacco. "I didn't know you smoked."

"Only at night when I can't sleep. If you're caught smoking dope here, they put you in jail."

She had taken a couple of hits off the toke John had rolled. It had been soggy. She didn't like feeling lightheaded, so she'd waved it away when Molly held it out to her again. "Well, it's no worse than smoking cigarettes," she said, standing on the porch, waiting to be excused.

"However lethal, cigarettes are legal." Josey waved a dismissive hand. "End of lecture."

And Annie went to bed. Whatever she dreamed that night, she forgot.

V

Josey

She crushed the cigarette and carried it inside, where she flushed it down the toilet in the first-floor bathroom. From upstairs she heard water running, then the opening of a door and the closing of another. Annie had gone to bed.

In her own bedroom, she pulled a sheet over herself and squeezed her eyes shut in hopes that sleep would come. When the clock read ten after three, she got up silently and dressed.

Downstairs, she wrote a note and left it for Annie to find on the kitchen table. She let the dog in the passenger side of the Escort and drove toward town. There was a cot in the back room at the Mill in case she got sleepy. She had spent nights there during the weeks prior to and after surgery before Annie came to live with her.

She parked in her usual spot, then went first to the dam to see the falls. The water glimmered under the stars and the lone street light that stood in front of the building.

Unlocking the front door, she walked through the darkened shop to the studio where she flipped the light switch and was nearly blinded by the track lighting under which she and Mary worked. Even the dog fell back with a whimper.

A blank sheet of art paper stood on an easel as it had for weeks. She sat in a chair and stared at it, then took a charcoal pencil and began sketching.

She had taken only quick glances at her image since studying it after the bandages came off, but she didn't need a mirror to know what she looked like. With quick strokes she outlined the upper half of a naked woman as seen in reflection. Shadows under the lone breast emphasized size and shape. She gave no dimension to the flattened skin where the other breast had been. The woman's mouth was slightly open in surprise or dismay, her eyes sunken in a gaunt face, her shoulders slightly slumped.

The windows lightened with the rising sun and rays streaked across the floor. She stood in front of the drawing, assessing it with an impartial eye. She envisioned this painting on canvas done in black and dark blue oils.

A tiredness flowed through her veins and she sat again on the folding chair, hungry and longing for a cigarette. At seven, she covered the easel with a clean sheet, left the dog behind, and walked to the Clover Coffee Shop.

Shelley Barnes approached her with a pad and pencil, ready to take her order. Shelley had been head cheerleader in high school, had upon graduation married Tom Barnes, the star quarterback, had given birth to a boy six months later and to four more sons in the ensuing years. Tom, who was supervisor of maintenance for the village, often joked that they had put together their own basketball team.

Shelley looked a little blowsy these days, with dyed blond hair the consistency of cotton candy. Her once slender frame carried too much weight. She was a cheerful person, though, who seemed content with her lot in life. Josey would bet that Shelley felt sorry for her, because she'd never married or produced any young.

"You look like you been up all night," Shelley said.

"I have. I need a cup of coffee. Bad."

While Shelley was pouring the black stuff into Josey's cup, Mary walked through the door.

"Hi, Shelley." Mary plunked down across from Josey and turned her cup over to be filled. "Fancy finding you here, Josey."

"When you're ready to order, give a holler."

"I want the stir fry breakfast," Josey said, pointing at the menu.

"I'll have the blueberry pancakes with American fries on the side." Mary handed back the menu without looking at it.

Shelley headed for the open window to the kitchen where she posted the orders. Mary lifted her cup and eyed Josey over the rim. "You look like you've been up all night."

"That's exactly what Shelley said." The coffee was strong, just what she needed. "I have."

"Why don't you ask the doctor for something to help you sleep?"

Josey shrugged. "When I see him next, I will."

They both glanced up as Ellen came through the door, followed by Roy.

Mary slammed her coffee cup in the saucer, hissing, "Don't let him sit with us."

Josey whispered back, "How am I going to do that?"

Before settling companionably between them, Roy pulled out a chair for Ellen and motioned her into it. "Aren't we lucky?"

"Maybe you'd like some privacy," Ellen said, looking from Mary to Josey.

"Don't leave." Mary grasped Ellen's wrist. "Josey and I are together all day. We don't need privacy."

"See, I knew they'd be glad to see us." Roy looked into Josey's face. "Are you okay?"

"If one more person comments on how I look . . ." Josey warned.

41

"Well, maybe you should go home and catch some z's," he advised.

"It's rude to tell someone she looks tired," Josey said, "So, enough. Okay?"

"Okay," he conceded, palms up. "Just showing my concern."

Shelley filled his and Ellen's coffee cups and took their orders.

Ellen looked uncomfortable, but not Roy. He leaned back in his chair and smiled broadly. "This is so nice, having breakfast with three of my favorite people."

"I'm having a small party Saturday afternoon. You're all invited," Ellen told them. "Come any time after three and stay as long as you like."

"How nice," Mary said. "What can I bring?"

"Yourselves. It's hospitality payback time."

"Excuse me a minute." Roy got up and headed for the men's room, stopping to chat on the way.

"I didn't mean to horn in on the two of you," Ellen said when he was out of earshot.

"You're not the one I don't want to see." Mary jerked her head meaningfully toward Roy who was at the back of the room. "He is."

Ellen was clearly embarrassed. "I didn't know. I hope you'll come on Saturday anyway."

Mary nodded. "Of course we will. Won't we, Josey?"

"Sure," Josey murmured, lifting her gaze from Ellen's V-necked blouse. She remembered how it felt to run a finger between those breasts and told herself she should be grateful not to be plagued by sexual need anymore. She never thought it would happen to her.

She met Ellen's eyes and was surprised by their intensity, a cobalt blue that bored into her. "Did you read the fishing mystery?"

"I read some of it last night. It didn't put me to sleep." She laughed at her little joke.

"She has a second mystery out when you're done with that one."

Shelley showed up with their plates, and Roy returned. Josey concentrated on her breakfast, her heart racing from the coffee and, she suspected, the lack of sleep.

Mary gave Josey a lift to the shop. "You are going to Ellen's get-together, aren't you?" Mary threw a glance at Josey.

"When I was young I felt sorry for Shelley, but then what did I know. Everything's so straightforward for her. Wouldn't that be nice?" she observed.

Mary said, "Tom's cheating on her. She just pretends it's not happening."

Josey was astonished. She unlocked the Mill and stepped inside, then bent to pat the dog who went bonkers with joy at their appearance. "How do you know that?"

"She told me. I think a lot of women make that choice. I won't." Mary walked into the back room with Josey and the dog on her heels. She stopped when she saw the covered easel. "You were painting last night, weren't you? Can I see?" She reached to remove the sheet.

Josey jumped forward. "No, not yet."

Mary turned a dark, solemn gaze on Josey. "I'm glad you're working again. I've been worried."

"Have you? Well, I'm worried about you. You don't want Roy to leave. You'd miss him terribly."

She went home early. Exhausted, she wanted only to fix a sandwich and fall into bed. Stopping to admire and follow Annie's paint job on the way into the house, she saw that the girl had continued on around the west side.

The girl was in the kitchen, stirring something on the stove. Sweat dampened her dark hair and beaded her upper lip. "I hope you like spaghetti."

"I like anything I don't have to fix," Josey said, dropping into a chair at the table, too tired to change the clothes that were sticking to her back. "You were busy today."

"Yep," the girl said. "This is Mom's recipe. I found all the ingredients in the pantry. Was that okay?"

"Of course." She leaned her chin on her hand and let the tiredness course through her. "You must need more paint."

"I do. I'll have to go to town tomorrow." Annie drained the spaghetti in a colander in the sink. Wreaths of steam enveloped her.

"How come you don't teach art?"

"Because I don't have a degree. If I did, I could be teaching rather than painting horses." How much better that would be she didn't know. She'd want to be at the tech or college level, which would require graduate courses. She'd have to live elsewhere.

"I'd pay to take your class. I don't care if you didn't finish college."

Josey sighed. "Save your money, Annie. Get that degree."

"I write," the girl said shyly. "One of my stories was printed in the university literary publication."

"Really? Congratulations."

"That was last winter." Annie shrugged. "Right now I'm writing a memoir. Actually, I've just started it."

"That'll keep you busy," Josey said, hoping she wouldn't be asked to read it. What would she say if it was terrible? But she felt duty-bound to ask to see the story.

"Sure. It's sort of autobiographical."

"So is painting sometimes," she said, thinking about the *Woman in Blue*, her title for the sketch she'd started in the early morning hours.

"Can I serve off the stove?"

"Good idea," Josey agreed, starting to get up, but Annie took her plate and filled it.

"I guess we're both artists in a way," the girl said, sitting down to eat.

Josey choked on a bite of salad, stifling a laugh. Had she been so brash in her youth? Opinionated, arrogant, yes, but unsure of her talent. It had taken years of moderate success before she'd thought of

44

herself as an artist. Perhaps the girl was just trying to warm up to her. She saw uncertainty in her every move.

They ate in relative silence. Josey was too tired to initiate any conversation. When Annie asked her questions, she replied in one or two words.

Josey was sitting on the porch in the warm evening when Annie gave her the bound booklet with her story in it.

"You don't have to comment," the girl said worriedly. "It's okay if you don't like it."

"Somebody liked it well enough to put it in print." A cardinal sang loudly from a nearby oak. Finding the index, she turned to the indicated page and began to read.

Nancy Nobody

Nancy was still in diapers when she realized she was nobody. Her stepfather never spoke to her, never touched her. He looked over her head, not at her, so that she grabbed her ears in fear and turned to see what was there. But there was never anyone, not even herself. Then he'd smile and turn his attention back to the TV or newspaper.

"Mama, Mama." Nancy pulled on her mother's white nursing slacks, looking for recognition.

Nancy's baby brother, Chad, lay on the bassinet, grabbing his pink feet and the spotlight. Her stepfather smiled at him over her mother's shoulder.

Her mother failed to respond to the tugging, and Nancy concluded that she wasn't there when her stepfather was, or that she was only there when he wasn't.

Josey looked up from the story, horrified by its implications, but Annie was nowhere to be seen.

Nancy was only naughty when she was alone with her mother and the baby. There was no point in vying for attention when her stepfather was around. Her mother would put a finger over her lips if she spoke in his pres-

45

ence, which made her think her mother didn't want him to know that she was there.

Instead, she sat on the couch and watched TV with him until it was time to eat or go to bed or something. Her brother crawled across the floor, grabbed her stepfather's pant leg, and was lifted onto his lap. There Chad would sit, smiling at Nancy, mocking her.

She couldn't hate her stepfather since he didn't know she existed, so she hated Chad. When no one was looking, she bonked him over the head or kicked him with her stocking feet.

That was how she got her stepfather to finally see her. She pushed Chad as he took his first steps in her direction, arms outstretched, and he fell and hit his forehead on the hearth.

Blood gushed out of the cut, and Chad howled his pain and hurt feelings. Nancy patted his back, horrified at what she'd done.

"You'll be fine," she said over and over.

Her stepfather knocked her out of the way. "What did you do to him, you little brat?" He yelled for her mother.

Her mother snatched her brother off the floor and dabbed at the wound with tissues taken from her pocket in a futile attempt to stop the bleeding. Squirming, Chad screamed louder. "This needs stitches," her mother said to her stepfather.

Nancy shrank into the corner, wanting to be invisible, but her mother called her to come with them. She climbed into the back seat of the car and fastened her seatbelt. Her mother held Chad in her arms in the front seat. Her brother was sobbing as if his heart was breaking.

"She pushed him," her stepfather said, backing out of the driveway.

"It was an accident," her mother insisted.

"She's a devil." The wheels squealed as the car took off.

Nancy looked out her window in surprise. Her stepfather knew she was there all along. She wasn't a nobody, she was something worse. She could tell from the tone of his voice. That's why he wouldn't look at her.

46

VI
Annie

Her aunt found her after reading her story and questioned her about it. "Were you Nancy?"

"I don't have a brother," she said. "I have three sisters, and I don't think he likes them any better than he likes me."

"Was it like that when you were a little kid? Was your mother like that?" Josey persisted.

"Naw. Mom loves me, and I never hurt my sisters. He wouldn't care if I did, so why do it?"

"Your story kept my attention. It's short, but good. Keep at it." Josey stared at her for a long moment with bloodshot eyes, then handed her the booklet. "I have to go to bed now. Are you going out?"

"Nope. I'm tired too." Painting in the hot sun all day after a late night had worn her out, but she wasn't going to bed before dark.

Elated by Josey's praise, however meager, she found it hard to concentrate on her book. Gnats joined the moths and a buzzing June bug in assaulting the overhead light and bats zipped around the yard in the growing dusk, while she squinted at the print. When the mosquitoes found her, she went inside.

Josey was gone when she got up the next morning, leaving another note on the kitchen table. The big house smelled of age and dust and spaghetti. Musty furniture lurked in the dark living and dining rooms. She felt lost in the space.

Propping her book open under a cutting board, she ate a bowl of cereal and two pieces of toast. She was close to the finish, more absorbed than ever in this strange, disturbing family. But she willingly put it down after eating, knowing that she had to go into town to get more paint.

Driving into Clover in a fog of excitement, holding silent, animated mental conversations with Molly, she felt deflated and foolish to find Molly's father behind the counter.

The paint can she carried hung forgotten in her hand. "Where's Molly?"

"Making deliveries. I'm her dad. What can I do for you?" He was short and compact with the physique of a much younger man.

"Oh." She put the empty can on the counter. "I need a couple more of these. They're for Josey Duprey."

"How's Josey these days?" he asked, moving the ladder to take the paint down.

"Fine," she replied, an easy assumption for her to make.

When she left, she said, "Say hello to Molly for me, will you? I'm Annie, Josey's niece."

In no hurry to paint she drove home slowly past fields filled with blue and orange and yellow wildflowers for which she had no names. Disappointment ached dully in her chest. She wondered if she'd always be hankering after some girl, always frustrated.

She'd been drawn to Sue her third year at the university in the same way she was to Molly. Sue's presence had brought out the funny, witty, attractive side of her that right now lay dormant. Once, when Josey had been lying on Sue's bed, she'd said something that made Sue tickle her. They'd ended up rolling around in a laughing tangle of legs and arms, finally falling to the floor. Josey had been electrified with hope that came to nothing. She had felt more alive when with Sue, just as she did now with Molly.

Parking the Jeep in front of the falling down garage, she carried the paint cans to the side of the house where she'd stopped yesterday. Here on the north side she was at least in the shade.

She opened the fresh can and began to apply the paint to the bare boards. On this side, where the sun never reached, there were no bushes or flowers to trample. Bare, cool sand lay underfoot.

She had fooled around with her friend, Lottie, her senior year of high school. They'd roomed together their first two years at the university, but their sexual relationship, such as it was, had ended rather abruptly when Lottie started going out with a nerdy guy. Secretly, Annie thought he was gay although she had yet to categorize herself that way. It had felt like a betrayal. Her fumbling sexual encounters with Lottie, beginning with kissing and ending with hesitant touching, had excited Annie in a way that no such acts with a boy ever had.

When Molly unexpectedly appeared around the side of the house, Annie was staving off the wish to masturbate. She'd heard a vehicle on the road but thought it had passed and stared at Molly with surprise.

"Dad said you'd stopped in for more paint." Molly took a few steps toward her, her hands in the back pockets of cut-off jeans. Her T-shirt clung to her in the heat. She looked terribly sexy to Annie. "I missed you at the store, so I thought I'd take a little delivery detour."

Annie wiped her forehead with her arm. "What time is it?" She'd put her watch in the pocket of her shorts.

"Almost noon." Molly smiled. "Want to take a break?"

"I was thinking about it."

They walked through the heat of midday to the side door. Annie felt less wasted than she had earlier in the week when she was working in its glare. She went straight to the bathroom, telling Molly to get something cold to drink out of the fridge.

Her face, throat, and neck were freckled with paint, and her right hand and wrist were thick with it. She eyed herself in the mirror as she washed and ran wet fingers through her dark mop of hair, entangling them in snarls.

Molly was sitting at the table, drinking a Pepsi, when she returned. She got a can out for herself and sat down with a thump. "Want a peanut butter and jam sandwich?" It was what she'd eaten for lunch every day since she came here.

Molly gave her a crooked smile, her brown eyes lighting up. "Sure."

She told herself she probably imagined the smile as sexy because of what she'd been thinking about when Molly appeared out of nowhere. She had transferred her sexual fantasies from Lottie, her only real-life experience, to Sue and now to Molly.

Making the sandwiches on paper plates at the counter, she carried them to the table. The stickiness of the thickly spread peanut butter was tempered and sweetened by the thin layer of jam. She closed her eyes with pleasure. When she opened them, she saw that most of Molly's sandwich was gone. "Want some chips?"

"You know what I really, really want?" Molly asked, her steady brown gaze giving Annie chills.

Annie choked a little on the peanut butter sticking to the roof of her mouth when she tried to speak. "What?" she finally managed.

"To take a little nap." Molly finished her last bite and took a swig of Pepsi without taking her eyes off Annie.

Annie felt a flush climb toward her face. "My bedroom's at the top of the stairs."

"With you. Doesn't the sun make you sleepy?" The brown eyes teased as a grin jerked at one corner of Molly's mouth.

"I wasn't in the sun," Annie said, unable to drop her gaze.

"Your face is red. Show me your room." Molly stood up and reached for Annie.

Molly's hand felt small and soft except for little calluses at the base of the fingers. Annie ran her thumb over these as she fought against being overwhelmed by the sudden, unexpected turn the visit had taken. Her breathing was ragged with fear and excitement. Her heart leaped around in her chest as if bent on escape. She led Molly up the stairs.

When Annie heard the bedroom door click shut behind them, she turned. Molly had closed the distance between them. Not daring to make the next move, she waited for Molly's lead.

"Come on. Lie down with me," Molly said, jerking her head toward the bed.

They lay for a few moments in the hot quiet, staring at the ceiling. Annie felt like a coiled spring, ready to be released by a word or touch.

Molly turned on her side. "Have you ever . . . with a girl?"

Annie gave a shrug open to interpretation. Maybe, yes, no, sort of. She turned her head to meet Molly's gaze.

"The thing is it's sort of like having sex without the worries."

"Worries?" Annie asked, mesmerized by Molly's eyes. Chocolate melting in the heat.

"You know. Your reputation being trashed. Risking pregnancy or some sexual disease. You can save yourself for the right guy."

Annie had never thought of sex with a girl in this way. It freed her of guilt, of responsibility, of possibly being a lesbian. She swallowed, her throat thick with desire.

"What do you say?"

"Say?" she repeated stupidly.

"Yes or no."

"Sure."

Molly leaned over her, her hair tickling Annie's nose.

Annie worried for a moment that her breath might be sour, but then she detected the odor of peanut butter and knew she smelled of

51

it, too. She concentrated on the kissing, wanting to remember the feel of Molly's soft lips crushed against her own, her warm tongue between her teeth.

Molly's hand slid down her and into Annie's shorts. They were an old pair that her aunt had given her to paint in and bagged at the waist and butt. The warm hand on her bare skin startled her into action, but she couldn't fit even her fingers inside the waist of Molly's shorts.

Molly unzipped Annie's shorts and tossed them on the floor, then pulled the T-shirt over Annie's head and dropped it. "Lie still," she said when Annie made a move to undress her.

Annie covered her bare breasts with her arms and kicked her tennis shoes off. Lying on the bedspread, wearing only panties, she watched Molly shed her outer clothing while kneeling on the bed. She felt terribly self-conscious and scrabbled back against the head rails of the bed, where she managed to slide between the sheets and cover herself.

Molly climbed in next to her in her underwear. Her hand closed over Annie's breast, encompassing it. "Nice," she said, giving Annie courage.

"Take this off, why don't you?" Annie asked, plucking at the sports bra.

They were awkward with each other. Annie knew she was fumbling, ascertaining the pleasure she gave by Molly's breathing. She touched Molly with awe at being allowed the privilege and felt immensely grateful that Molly seemed to want her. In her own eyes she had always been lacking. Her breasts and bottom were too small, her nose too big, her skin too pale, her ears too large. She thought Molly perfectly proportioned with smooth, olive skin.

When it was quickly over, they lay side by side again, eyes on the ceiling. Panting from the heat of their bodies and the afternoon, Annie's heart thudded a little less erratically. She wondered when and if they would do this again but afraid to ask, she said nothing.

Molly glanced at her watch. "Oh my god, I've got to get going.

Dad'll kill me." She turned her back to Annie and struggled into her bra and panties, then got up and put on the rest of her clothes. "Where's the john?"

"Down the hall." Annie pointed. When Molly left the room, she hurriedly dressed.

Following Molly outside, she watched her drive off, tires spewing sand. Then she went back inside to look at herself again in the mirror, this time to see if she appeared any different. She felt changed. Her cheeks glowed brightly, her eyes glittered, her mouth was redder and fuller.

Upstairs, she tidied the bed before going back outside to paint. Molly had said nothing about seeing her again, and she chewed this around worriedly for a while. Then she relived over and over what they had done together. It had been a vast improvement over her episodic sex with Lottie. When she walked, she tingled between her legs.

Her heart expanded with what she was sure was love for Molly. She knew she'd live in limbo until she saw her once more. Since they'd not spoken of it during or after, she had no idea how Molly felt, which caused an anxiety that she knew would grow with the passing days.

VII
Josey

Josey had left for the Mill just as the first hint of sunrise spread across the horizon. Shades of pink stained the emergence of blue. The dog panted at her side, shifting excitedly in his seat. It was how she felt, eager to get there, to paint the drawing on canvas.

It wasn't until she'd sped past a woman standing in the ditch by the road that she recognized Ellen in the rearview mirror. She knew Ellen was gathering fresh wildflowers for the library or for home. Some people would call them weeds, but Ellen claimed the only weeds were invasive plants, ones that drove out the native ones, and some of those had the most beautiful blooms. Like purple loosestrife.

She was driving past the trailer park where Ellen had recently rented a mobile home from someone who spent winters in Florida. Ellen had already given notice on her apartment, the plan being to move in with Josey, when Josey had copped out.

Waving through the partially open window, she saw Ellen raise a hand before she receded from sight. Turning at the stop sign onto Main Street—there were no stoplights in Clover—she drove past the maintenance building as Tom Barnes pulled out in the opposite direction. He stuck a big hand out the window of the town's pickup and she fluttered hers in greeting, liking him even if he was cheating on Shelley.

Except for the hum of the old fridge they kept in the studio, the Mill was cool and quiet. Flicking on the track lighting, she lifted the sheet from the sketch. A little thrill, such as she'd not felt since before the surgery, seized her.

Engrossed in what she was doing, she jumped when the dog scrabbled for traction and rushed toward the door. She covered her work and went into the shop. Through the small pane of leaded glass, she made out Roy's contorted features and opened up to him.

"I saw your Escort out there. Are you all right?"

"Yeah, I'm fine. What are you doing up so early?"

"Mary changed the locks yesterday. I slept in my truck." Wrinkled and unshaven, he looked it.

"Come on in." She locked the door behind him. "I've got the coffee on."

"I don't know what to do anymore," he muttered, accepting the cup she handed him.

"Find your own place, Roy," she said, exasperated with his obdurate refusal to see things as they were. "Get on with your life and let Mary get on with hers."

He slumped in the chair behind the counter where Buddy nosed his hand for a pat. "All my money's invested in the log home I'm building in Barkins Woods; I'll move in when it's done." He looked up at her with pleading eyes. "I know this is a lot to ask, but can I stay with you till then?"

"No, absolutely not. Mary would never forgive me." Her first loyalty, after all, was to Mary. "Why can't you sleep at the office?" She'd seen it. There was furniture, a fridge, a stove, even a television. "It's furnished."

"The manufacturer owns it, and it always has to be clean enough for the public."

"It's just for the short term," she said, only wanting to get back to work before Mary showed up.

"All right. You're heartless, and I'm out of here." He gave Buddy another pat and got up. "You'll be sorry for not taking me in. I cook, I clean, I mow the grass, I wash clothes."

"Probably," she agreed, "but I have to work with Mary."

She ushered him out the door, saying, "This will give you incentive to get the loghouse finished," and returned to her canvas.

When she got home that evening, the colored horse prints were among the mail Annie had placed on the kitchen table. They were good. She was studying them with a critical eye, sure that even Bud Lovelace would approve, when Annie came down the stairs, her hair still wet from the shower.

The girl glanced over Josey's shoulder. "Wow. That's the horse?"

"Yep, that's Monty."

"You take good pictures."

"Thanks. I think I'll give the Lovelaces a call and see if they want to look at the prints. Care to come along?"

They left the dog sitting forlornly in the dusty driveway and drove off in Annie's Jeep. Josey's hair whipped against her forehead and cheeks, sometimes reaching her eyes. She'd forgotten what it was like to ride in an open vehicle.

They parked in front of the Lovelace barn where they sat in the Jeep until John put the doberman in a stall.

Bud passed the prints on to his wife and son. "How much for all of them?"

"I need them for the painting. Which one would you like me to draw from, or do you want me to take more photos?" She'd brought her camera.

"Can you blow up these prints instead? These are really good."

"How about a portrait of his head, Dad, to put above the fire-place?" John stood near Annie on the other side of the Jeep.

"We contracted for a painting, Bud, not for photos. Let's choose from one of these," Brenda said.

Josey hadn't expected Bud Lovelace to back out of the deal. She told him a portrait would cost five hundred dollars over the phone and he snapped it up. She was glad she hadn't priced the photos yet. "I'll sell you the prints after the portrait's done."

"Can you do a painting of his head from these?"

"Sure."

"I'm going to show Annie the horses," John said, and they disappeared into the stable's interior, leaving Josey standing in the drive with Brenda and Bud.

"I hope you weren't about to sit down to dinner," she said to Brenda.

"We never eat till the stalls are cleaned and the horses fed," Bud said. "Business first."

She hadn't thought of horses as money makers, but as more of a hobby. "I don't want to keep you from your work. I'll just wait here for Annie."

Brenda coaxed, "Come into the barn. You can wait in the office if you want."

The wall of windows in the air-conditioned office faced an indoor riding arena. A radio softly played country music. Josey paged through issues of *The Quarter Horse Journal*, finding an advertisement for Lovelace Quarter Horses and Monty, whose real name was Montana Joe King.

Glancing at her watch, she decided to look for her niece when John led Monty into the arena. She went into the arena herself to get a better look at the horse.

"Why don't you take him outside and let me get some shots of his head?" Josey suggested. "And then we better go, Annie."

After the photo session, they left. Conversation was not an option with the wind echoing in their ears. Bouncing down their sandy drive, Annie parked next to Roy's F250 four-wheel-drive truck.

Roy looked up from opening a bottle of Bogle Merlot as they entered the house. The table was set for three. A large salmon fillet, sprinkled with dill, lay on the broiler pan on top of the stove. A bowl filled with salad greens and thin slices of red peppers stood on the table. Dressing, sour cream, and sliced lemon were nearby. Three potatoes sat in the microwave, waiting to be nuked.

Josey swallowed a smile at the modest repast in the making. Mary had told her that Roy made most of the meals, but food meant little to Mary. It was sustenance so that she could work. Josey loved to eat much more than she liked to cook.

Roy put the salmon under the broiler and pushed the button on the microwave. "Trying to worm my way into your affections, of course. I wondered where you were when only Buddy greeted me."

Before Roy could pour the wine, Josey said, "It won't work, Roy."

"How about a toast for this young woman who's come to live in Clover?" he said.

"This young woman is here because she was at an underage drinking party. Don't tempt her."

"It's okay," Annie said, looking confused and amused at the same time. "I don't like wine."

"Just as well. No need to start trying," Josey said.

"Spoken like an aunt." Roy winked at the girl. "My name is Roy, and you are Josey's niece?"

"Annie," the girl said.

Feeling temporarily defeated, Josey sat down. "We were at Lovelaces', showing them photos of their stallion. Do you know Bud and Brenda?"

"I built their house. He nickeled and dimed me. Better get your money in advance."

"I'll hang onto the portrait till I do."

"Someone get the potatoes. Dinner's ready." He took the salmon out.

Eyeing the fish as he cut it into three pieces, Annie said, "I don't know if I can eat that much."

"This girl is ripe for culinary exploration. Where's the grill, Josey? I'm an expert griller."

"I don't grill," Josey told him, "so there is none. Even if the food is superb, we're not making this a habit. Hear? You eat at your house, we'll eat at ours."

"You're as bad as Mary. She'll probably suffer from malnutrition without me around to feed her." He looked at Annie as she picked at the salmon on her plate. "Do you like it?"

"It's great," Annie took a bigger bite. "We never had fish at home, because my stepfather didn't like it."

After dinner, Roy pushed his chair back. "I thought I'd look at the garage."

"I'll come with you," Josey said warily. "Do you mind if we leave you with the dishes, Annie?"

Annie had already started cleaning up. "Nope. I do this part real well."

The dog tagged along after a look of longing at the empty plates being rinsed in the sink. The evening was warm and still. The grass, seared by the heat, crunched underfoot.

"You could use some repairs around here. A big wind might push the garage over."

She knew that was an exaggeration, albeit a slight one. The boards were rotting where there should have been a foundation. "When I can afford repairs, I'll call you."

"I could get my backhoe in here, jack this up, and put a foundation under it."

"You're not moving in," she said firmly, even though sorely tempted.

"Want a cigarette?" He shook one out of the pack in his pocket.

"I shouldn't," she hedged.

"Neither should I," he agreed as they both lit up.

59

She rode with Mary to Ellen's party Saturday afternoon. Mary closed the doors as soon as the last customers departed around four. Josey had told her that Roy wanted to move in with her and Annie.

Zipping out of the parking lot, pausing only briefly to look for coming traffic, she said, "He's an expert at getting his way. Remember who's your best friend."

"You are," Josey said tensely, as an oncoming driver slammed on brakes and blew the horn. "Don't kill us, please. I would have told you sooner, but I knew you'd be upset."

"Were you even thinking of taking him in?"

"Absolutely not. Those were my words, even though he said he'd put a foundation under the garage."

"Are you trying to make me feel guilty?"

"No. Maybe. I don't know. I don't want to get in the middle. Okay?"

"I knew you wouldn't capitalize on my loss," Mary said, affirming what she'd just questioned.

"It wasn't your loss. It was your choice," she pointed out.

Mary heaved a sigh and said gloomily, "A bitter one."

Josey couldn't resist saying, "Martyrdom doesn't suit you," as Mary slipped the Taurus neatly between two vehicles on the curb in front of Ellen's trailer.

The trailer was a double-wide with a three-season porch in the front and a deck out back. Lights were strung from the trees, and music played from a CD player plugged into an outlet on the deck. Rented tables and chairs crowded the deck and lawn beyond. A privacy fence surrounded the backyard.

Ellen greeted them a little distractedly, enough so that Josey felt snubbed. Her sunbleached blond curls, which Josey knew to be natural, had gone frizzy in the humidity. Enlarged pupils blackened her blue eyes, sunburn or excitement tinged her cheeks pink. She wore shorts and a boat-necked T-shirt that clung to her in the heat.

Josey found her eyes gravitating toward Ellen's breasts. She had no interest in sex, yet she recalled clearly the last time they had made love. Lying on smooth sheets in Ellen's apartment, they had spoken of Ellen's move to Josey's house.

She knew she'd behaved badly when she'd abruptly aborted their plans to live together, but Ellen had seemed to take it in stride. "That's okay, Josey," she'd said when Josey used Annie's moving in as an excuse. "I'd rather know now."

"If you can't find a place to live . . ." Josey had said.

"That's not a problem. I'll let you know where I am."

Now Josey looked around the yard and spotted Shelley and Tom Barnes along with a host of other townspeople. Roy was not among them.

"Go on inside and get something to drink and eat," Ellen said, turning away to meet someone else.

They climbed the steps to the deck and went in through the sliding patio screen door. Filling plates from the food on the extended kitchen table and pouring wine from the bottles on the counter, Josey and Mary wandered into the living room.

All the chairs were taken. After stopping to exchange a few words with others, they went back out on the deck and sat at one of the tables. Josey found herself following Ellen with her eyes.

Shelley came over and sat with them. "Nice party. I feel like I should be taking orders, though." She laughed, her gaze on Tom who was talking with the police chief, Bernie Protheroe.

Josey overcame the urge to place a comforting hand on Shelley's arm. "It's okay," she wanted to say, although how could it be?

"How are the boys?" Mary asked, her eyes on the entrance gate to the backyard. Josey knew she was trying not to look for Roy.

"Just about grown and gone," Shelley said, not at all sadly. "I hardly ever see them anymore. I thought that would bother me, but it doesn't. I'm too busy."

Roy must have come in the front door, because he suddenly

appeared at their table carrying a plate crammed with food, a beer in his other hand. "Got room for me?"

Mary gave him a hard look. "You can have my seat."

"We can't even be friends," he muttered, watching her go. "There's no pleasing her."

Ellen brought a tall, handsome woman to their table and introduced her as Helen Griswold, an old school friend who had driven over from La Crosse and was spending the weekend. The two sat briefly with them before excusing themselves and wandering off to another table.

Josey watched them go, sure that she had been replaced in Ellen's life. When the evening ended after midnight, she felt as if her thanks went hardly heeded. The inattention annoyed her. Mary had left earlier, and Roy took Josey to the Mill in his truck so that she could drive home.

VIII
Annie

John called late Saturday afternoon as Annie moped around the house. He picked her up in the evening in his battered Bronco and drove her to the Gray Fox. She'd neither seen nor talked to Molly since their lovemaking. She'd been to the hardware store to pick up paint and asked Molly's dad to tell Molly hello. Maybe he'd forgotten. More likely Molly had chosen to ignore what had happened between them.

"It isn't fancy, but it's mine," he said.

"Well, it's a Cadillac compared to my Jeep," she replied absently, so nervous about seeing Molly that she felt she might throw up any minute.

They drove into the crowded parking lot. John fitted the Bronco between two pickups. "At least I don't have to worry about adding a few more dents to this."

"Seems like everyone's got a four-wheel drive here," she remarked.

"We're northern rednecks," John said, getting out.

She stood outside the bar for a moment, fighting an urge to flee, but there was nothing for her to run away in. John held the door open for her.

Assaulted by smoke and noise, she scanned the crowd through squinting eyes. John took her arm and led her to the bar where he ordered a couple of beers. She hardly heard what he was shouting at her, so busy was she looking for Molly. Her heart thumped in her ears when she thought she spied her, but the girl turned and became someone else.

"Let's take these outside," he said, bandying remarks with the young people they passed.

Sitting on a picnic table on the deck, John talked about leaving for a four-day horse show in another state on Sunday. "Today I spent all day getting two horses ready."

"How do you get a horse ready? What do you have to do?" she asked, focusing on those milling around inside the wall of windows.

"Clip ears and bridle paths and fetlocks, thin manes, clean gear, get the trailer ready. Tomorrow I'll get up around dawn and wash Monty and the mare I'm taking. Have you ever been to a quarter horse show?"

"Nope." In fact, she hadn't been aware there was such a thing nor had she cared.

"It's like a whole different world. These people live and breathe horses."

"Yeah?" she asked, trying to put some interest in her voice. He seemed to like her and she needed a friend, but she found it impossible to dispel the funk she'd fallen into.

"Yeah." He was looking at her, one hand on his knee. "You okay?"

She roused herself. "Sorry. I feel like a slug."

"Who are you looking for in there?"

"Just trying to put faces and names together." It wasn't exactly a lie.

"They'll stick after a while."

That was when she spotted Molly, emerging from the crowd, looking out the windows, melting back into the throng. Her heart jerked painfully. She swallowed her disappointment, sure that Molly had seen her.

Gulping down the beer, she set the bottle on the table. "Let's walk down to the lake."

"You're not much of a drinker," he said as they left the lighted deck. The night closed around them, black to her unaccustomed eyes.

"Bad experience," she muttered. As her eyes adjusted to the dark, she picked out the differing shades of sand and water, trees and grass. They walked past the clutter of paddle boats, a jutting pier, the end of the swimming area marked by buoys. John took her hand. His was dry and hard.

They passed a number of cottages and an assortment of piers and boats. The sound of croaking and chirping grew louder until it filled her ears. "Are those frogs?" she asked.

"Yep. They're making tadpoles. There's a little swamp down here where the overflow from the lake goes." He stopped and she saw the marsh grass. "We'll have to take off our shoes to go on."

She pulled off her sandals and waded into the warm shallows. Her chest ached whenever she thought of Molly turning away from her. She was sure Molly was sorry and probably ashamed about what had happened. It didn't matter that Molly had initiated the sex. Nothing mattered.

John caught up with her and took her hand again. "Do you miss the big city?"

"No." She could never wade in Lake Michigan at night like this. Never mind the cold water and lack of good places to wade, it wouldn't be safe.

They walked the circumference of the lake, splashing in the water past beach fires with cottage owners sitting around the flames. The water belonged to everyone, John told her. Everyone they met greeted them in a friendly fashion.

It was a small lake, and they were back where they'd begun before Annie was ready to be. She'd almost convinced herself that Molly hadn't seen her on the deck, but she wasn't confident enough yet to confront Molly. Hanging back a little as they trudged up to the deck through the sand, she said, "I think I'll wait out here."

"Okay. I'll get a couple of beers." Oblivious to her inner turmoil, he went inside. She sat on the picnic table they'd occupied earlier.

She saw him at the bar, talking to friends, making his way back toward the deck. It was wall-to-wall people, and she lost sight of him for a few minutes. When he emerged, Molly and the same young man she'd left on the beach the other night were with him.

Annie's heart banged around inside her chest, a buzzing filled her ears, and she struggled to breathe normally. She was filled with conflicting emotions. Thrilled that Molly was acknowledging her, jealous of the guy at her side, terrified of finding out somehow that Molly thought their sexual epidsode a terrible mistake.

"Look who I found," John said, handing Annie the foam filled, icy glass.

Annie's smile trembled a little and then disappeared altogether. "Hi, Molly." And to the young man at her side, "Sorry. I'm terrible at names."

"Rob Casperson. Cass. And you? I can't remember names either."

"Annie."

"You one of the locals or do you have a cottage around here?" Cass asked.

"Neither. I'm spending the summer with my aunt. I'm from Milwaukee. And you?"

"His dad has a new place on Evergreen Lake. Roy Schroeder built it," Molly said.

"Do you feel like you're in the backwoods sometimes?" Cass flashed a toothy grin at Molly. "Charming country, though."

If she hadn't already disliked him because of his interest in Molly, she would have found him offensive for this snobbish remark. "Not at all. Where are you from? Chicago?"

"Nope. Oshkosh."

"That's not exactly big city, is it?"

"Big enough," he said, downing his beer. He threw Molly an inquiring look.

"How are you, Molly?" Annie asked. "You haven't been in the store much."

Molly looked uncomfortable. "I know. I've been out on deliveries."

Annie bit her lip and looked away, trying for anger. She felt instead like crying.

Cass cleared his throat. "Well, I think I'll get another beer. Anybody else?"

"I'll come with you," Molly said. "See ya."

John watched them go with a puzzled frown. "Who the hell does he think he is?"

Annie shrugged, too disheartened to comment. "I don't feel so hot." In fact, she felt nauseated.

"I'll take you home."

"You have to get up at dawn anyway," she pointed out, more miserable because he was so nice and she was spoiling his evening.

The next day she slept late and would have stayed in bed all day had it not been so hot and her room so bright. Josey had been gone when John brought her home the night before, and she was gone when Annie got up.

She pulled on the shorts and T-shirt she'd dropped on the floor and dragged herself downstairs. The note on the kitchen table said that Josey had gone to the mill. The dog was with her.

Disheartened, Annie opened the humming fridge and pulled out the milk and orange juice. Sitting at the table with the Sunday paper, she ate a bowl of honey oats and a piece of toast.

When someone knocked on the door, her heart leaped, but Roy was on the other side, not Molly.

"I dropped my hundred-foot tape out by the garage and Josey found it and put it inside." He looked at her as she retreated to the table and hunched over her cereal. "Rough night?" he asked with lofted brows.

She shrugged, not even caring how she looked. "No. How was the party?"

"Okay. How was the Gray Fox? Shoulder-to-shoulder kids?"

"Yeah. We walked around the lake."

"It was a nice night for that. You made it home before we did."

"John had to get up at the crack to go to a horse show."

"Oh, yes, the super horse." He shot a glance at her. "Why so glum? Did you want to go with him?"

"God, no. I don't like horses."

"Why's that?" He looked interested.

"One ran away with me once." She remembered her manners. "Want some coffee?"

"Sure."

She poured from the half-full pot Josey had left and put the cup in the microwave."

He scooped up his tape and leaned against the counter. "I keep all confidentialities, and sometimes I even give good advice."

She looked into his eyes and tried to smile, but it hurt her face.

"Come on, honey. Cough it up. You can tell me anything. I've heard it all."

She said miserably, "I don't want to talk about it."

"Maybe another time. It's too early for true confessions anyway." He downed the coffee and let himself out the door. She heard his truck cough to life.

While idly paging through the Sunday paper and sipping luke-warm coffee, she wondering what she would do with this day. She might as well paint. John was out of town, and Molly was never going to call or come over on her own.

Startled when the phone rang. she shuffled over to answer it. "Hello. Oh hi, Mom. How are you?"

"Okay, honey. How's the house coming?"

"Pretty good."

"I'm coming over for your birthday next weekend. Is Josey there?"

In her wretchedness she'd forgotten her birthday. She'd be twenty-one. Legal. "No, she's at the Mill. They're open Saturdays and Sundays."

"Maybe she could take some time off. I'll be there before noon on Saturday. Okay? Have you got any plans?"

"Not me. I don't have plans. How are my little sisters?"

"Sassy. We'll talk next weekend. Okay?"

She hung up and dragged her feet back to the table. Brightening a little, she realized that no one could arrest her for having a beer.

IX
Josey

Josey went to the Mill Sunday morning around five o'clock. She felt as if she hadn't slept in weeks, but she awoke every morning now as the sun peeked over the horizon and knew there was no point in staying in bed. She had left the dog on the front porch and a note on the table.

She was at work on the *Woman in Blue* when she heard a noise behind her, and turned. Mary stood there, her dark eyes wide, her hand over her mouth.

"You snuck up on me," she said, aggrieved and alarmed. "Well?"

"It's wonderful. Too good to sell to someone to put in their house."

"It's not finished yet," Josey said, pleased despite herself.

"It's the best thing you've done." Mary studied the painting a while longer. Then, "It makes me want to cry."

Josey remembered the nights she'd spent crying and said nothing.

Mary put an arm around her and rested her head on Josey's shoulder. She smelled wonderful, a combination of herself and shampoo and cologne and soap. "You can't hide this painting from everyone."

Josey said, hoping it was so, "It could be of anyone."

Studying Josey close-up, Mary asked, "I can understand why you don't want the general public to know, but why not Ellen?"

"I don't want pity. And I don't want to talk about it."

"Why would she pity you?"

"I can't test her feelings right now. Give me time."

Mary drew away, her eyes searching Josey's. "So when is the appointment with the plastic surgeon again?"

"July thirtieth, but it's just to talk about reconstruction and set a date for surgery. I can do that alone."

"Why don't you work today? I'll tend the shop. Are you hungry? You look kind of skinny, Josey."

"Coffee. I'll run over to the coffee shop and get a bagel to go."

"I'll get it. Be right back."

Josey turned back to the painting. Every other thought fell away.

When Mary returned with two bagels smeared thickly with cream cheese, she ate with one hand and worked with the other.

Late in the afternoon she heard Ellen's voice, slapped a sheet over the painting, and went to the door to the shop. Ellen's friend, Helen, was with her.

Josey took the woman in with her eyes. Slender, with more silver than black in her hair, smooth-skinned, Helen stood out in a crowd. Stepping forward, she shook hands. "Another visit?"

Helen smiled, her face falling into friendly planes, her hazel eyes lighting up. "It's Ellie's turn next time."

"You should have brought Helen in sooner, Ellen," Josey said.

"I don't know why she didn't," Helen agreed. "This is a wonderful gallery. Is the work all yours and Mary's?"

Josey exchanged a look with Mary. "Yes. Mary is the potter. I'm the painter."

Before leaving, Helen bought one of her paintings and two of Mary's pottery pieces, making it hard for Josey to dislike her. However, every time Helen called Ellen Ellie, Josey found it easier. After the door closed behind them, Josey asked, "Well? Are they or aren't they?"

"Hard to tell. Maybe they're just good friends."

"Exchanging weekends at each other's homes? Come on, Mary."

"Do you care?" Mary raised one eyebrow when she asked questions.

Did she? "Some. Do you think she's prematurely gray?"

"Definitely. Not enough wrinkles. They're probably old school chums."

At home Buddy met her as she got out of the Escort and walked around the garage. A backhoe sat next to the garage, which was raised on jacks. A trench had been excavated under it, the sandy soil deposited behind the building.

She found Roy and Annie on the porch, he with a bottle of ale and Annie with a diet Pepsi. Roy wore torn shorts and a dirty T-shirt. Annie looked much the same, only a little cleaner.

"I can't pay for that, Roy." She pointed in the direction of the garage.

"Now before you get all worked up, let me explain. It needed doing. The garage was going to topple over."

"I can't even begin to pay. Besides, those kind of decisions are mine to make."

His burned face was smudged with dirt. "Sue me, then."

"I just might." The presumptuousness of what he'd done collided with her gratitude.

"Want me to finish it or not?" He let his feet fall to the floor with a clunk.

"Well, you can't just leave it that way."

He got up and started toward his truck, mumbling something about not being appreciated.

"I'll pay for the cement," she hollered after him. He waved an arm without turning.

Annie and the dog followed Josey inside. The screen door slapped behind them. "Mom's coming next Saturday. For my birthday. She called."

"Your birthday?" She'd forgotten. Maybe she'd show Liz the painting. They were fraternal twins, as different as any sisters might be, but Liz had always shown an interest in Josey's art.

Mary was after her to put the painting on the wall with a Not for Sale sign under it when it was finished. Josey told her she was going to do a before-the-mastectomy painting to contrast with the *Woman in Blue*. The two would have to be paired. Exhibiting either, even at the Mill, would have to wait for both to be done.

When she and Annie sat down to eat, she was pondering the complexion and expression of the next painting. Should it be the Woman in Red? Should the woman be smiling or should she look wistful as if she knew of the impending mastectomy? Maybe they both should be titled *Woman in the Mirror*.

Annie said quietly, "It's none of my business, I know, but I thought Roy meant well."

Jolted out of her train of thought, she stared at her niece for a moment before saying, "You're right, Annie. It is none of your business." She thought she spoke gently enough.

Annie ducked her head as if to hide her flush from Josey.

"Look," Josey said, "no one, no matter how well meant, should take it upon himself to make my decisions for me. How would you like it if I enrolled you in some college without asking?"

Annie shrugged and murmured, "I guess I wouldn't."

That night Monty galloped into Josey's dreams, skidding to a halt nearly in her face so that she awakened in a sweat of fear. The sky was just beginning to lighten. She lay quietly, realizing she'd have to put aside the *Woman in Blue* in favor of Monty's portrait.

That morning she began to sketch Monty's head from a photograph. Mary stood behind her. "Pretty horse. He looks more like a mare than a stud."

"He's a ladies' man." She turned to look at Mary. "Liz is coming this weekend. Can we trade Friday and Monday for Saturday and part of Sunday?"

"Sure. Are you going to tell her?"

"I thought I'd bring her in and show her the painting." She put aside the urge to tell Mary about the garage. It would only stir up Mary's indignation.

The week sped by. Tuesday, Thursday, and Friday Josey spent in the gallery shop. Traffic was slow on weekdays. At Mary's suggestion she set up the easel with Monty's portrait near the shop windows so that she could work on it. Mary said it would be good advertising for her portrait business.

Ellen came in shortly before noon on Friday with the second fishing mystery. Josey had finished the first one and dropped it in the outdoor slot at the library on Monday. Ellen also brought three bagels and cream cheese to share, along with a deli macaroni salad. It reminded Josey of earlier days, when Ellen came over for lunch every day, when the three of them took turns providing it.

"Come on out and eat," Ellen called to Mary.

Mary emerged from the studio. "Thanks. I'm absolutely starved."

"Me, too," Josey concurred, as Ellen placed the food on the counter. She experienced a moment of keen regret for letting Ellen go, but thought maybe Ellen had already been slipping away.

"Going to Helen's house this weekend, Ellen?" Mary asked.

Ellen nodded, swallowing a bite of bagel. "When the library closes on Saturday."

"That's a long hike," Mary went on.

"It is, but it's lovely over there. She has a boat on the Mississippi. She fishes. I read."

Josey said nothing. As a high school teacher, Helen had her weekends and summers free and a boat on top of that. Josey worked seven days a week and lived on the edge. She could not compete with Helen.

With a nod toward the portrait, Ellen said, "The horse is wonderful, Josey. Such soulful eyes."

"Thanks, from me and Monty."

"What are you two up to this weekend?" Ellen asked.

"I have to work. Josey's twin sister, Liz, is coming to visit."

"Does your niece like it here?"

"I don't really know. All I know is it's her twenty-first birthday, and she's painting my house for her keep." She'd pick one of her paintings as a gift for Annie.

"How far back do you and Helen go?" Mary asked.

Ellen brightened. "High school. When we get together, it's like we've never been apart. We talk and talk."

When Ellen left, Mary said, "Go after her. Tell her about the mastectomy, explain why you didn't want her to know."

"No," Josey said flatly. "I can't."

"Then let me." Mary edged toward the door.

"Absolutely not."

When Liz arrived Saturday morning, Josey was out in the garden weeding. She had awakened at dawn and gone into the Mill to work on the *Woman in Blue* until nine. She walked toward Liz's car, straightening and limbering up as she went. Buddy beat her there.

"Hello, sis." She never realized how much she missed Liz until she saw her again. Liz was her other half. The one who remembered the part of their growing up that she'd forgotten. She hugged her sister, feeling the tension in her body. "Hey, relax. You're in the boonies now as Annie would say."

Smiling distractedly, Liz shot a look down the driveway toward the road. "How is Annie?"

"She got all the way around the house this week as far as she can reach from the ground. It's primer so it's spotty."

"I was a little worried about her. She was so shook up by that boy's death. Said she was never going to drink again. I suppose that lasted about two days."

"That's about right."

Liz looked at the garage on jacks and the freshly poured foundation. "Who did this?"

Josey's lips tightened. "Roy Schroeder, as an unasked favor. I'm paying for the cement."

"Have you gone straight on me?" Liz asked, her arm around Josey's waist as they headed toward the house.

"Don't you wish. Remember Mary, my business partner? Well, he's her husband. They're separated. He just went ahead and did this on his own." She gestured at the garage.

"Nice of him," Liz said absently, glancing again behind her.

"A little nervy, I thought. What is it, Lizzie? Are you expecting someone?"

"Charles might show up to get the Jeep."

"Nice birthday present for Annie," Josey said as anger swept through her. Charles couldn't let her or Annie enjoy a weekend with Liz without butting in.

X
Annie

She hugged her mother, fighting off the urge to melt into her, then tucked her hands in the back pockets of her cut-offs. "How come you didn't bring my sisters?"

"Your dad didn't want *me* to come," her mother said. "Happy birthday, sweetie."

"He's not my dad, Mom." She followed her mother's nervous glance toward the driveway and felt uneasy. "Does he know how to get here?"

Her mother's smile quivered in the corners. "He hasn't forgotten, I'm sure."

Annie said, "Come on in, Mom. I'll get you some iced tea."

Annie filled three glasses and sat down with her mother and Josey. "Fill me in on what's going on at home." She felt as if she'd been cut off from her former life and listened raptly with chin on hand.

After Annie's mother fell silent, Josey said, "I thought we'd go into the Mill after lunch today. I have something to show you, Lizzie."

Annie's hopes lifted. "I'll get more paint while you do that." Maybe Molly would be at the hardware store. She hadn't seen her all week.

"Why don't we all go for a walk this morning?" Josey suggested. "I haven't shown Annie the path through the woods to the pond."

The dog ran in front of them, joy in his every move. Annie took up the rear, her eyes on the needle strewn path. When her mother stopped suddenly, she nearly bumped into her. Josey was pointing at a lump in one of the pines. Looking closely, Annie saw a tiny owl peering back, then its head swiveled ninety degrees and she was looking at its back.

After that, she kept her eyes up and caught the flash of red and black as a Baltimore oriole flew across the pathway, saw a doe flag its tail and bound away.

"Her fawn is probably lying down somewhere nearby," Josey said as Annie stood in thrall at these glimpses of wildlife.

The woods in front of them opened up, revealing a small pond. It reflected the trees and sky in its blue surface. Reeds grew around the edges. Buddy dashed through these into the water where he floundered after ducks. Squawking loudly, wings flapping, skimming the surface in their rush to get away, yet unwilling to leave their babies behind, they fled in front of his assault.

Josey called the dog back and the ducks settled down to a steady scolding from a safe distance. She took off her shoes and waded along the edge of the pond, and Annie and her mother did the same.

"Like when we were kids, Josey," Annie's mother said.

"Do you miss the place, Lizzie?"

Her mother nodded. "Of course, I do."

Flies buzzed around their heads. Annie was glad she had her Ace Hardware cap on. Josey had lent her mother a straw hat and put one on herself before leaving the house. Buddy snapped in irritation at the pests.

The sun lay warm on her shoulders. The water cooled her feet only slightly. She would have put her face to the sky, except for the flies.

Josey put her shoes back on. She pointed across the pond to a tall, crane-like bird that took flight, tucking its long neck into an **S**. "A great blue heron."

Annie swatted and squinted into the sun.

Josey looked at her watch. "Time to go back. We can have lunch and head into town."

"Let's eat lunch out. My treat," Annie's mother said.

"Fine with me." Josey smiled, and Annie thought how much they looked alike.

Josey insisted on driving. The tables in the restaurant were all taken, and they sat at the counter to order.

Shelley passed out menus. "Liz! Good to see you."

"Good to be here."

They ordered and moved to a vacated table in the far corner. When Shelley stopped to see how they were doing, her mother asked, "How's Tom?"

Tight-lipped, Shelley shrugged. "Okay, I guess."

"Tell him hello for me."

"I will, when I see him." Shelley moved on.

Annie's mother asked Josey in a low voice, "What's going on with Tom?"

Josey shook her head. "I don't know."

Her mother then looked at her worriedly.

"What is it?" she asked.

"Your dad wants the Jeep, honey. He may show up with Jeanne to drive it back."

"How will I get around?" She heard her voice skittering high with complaint. She'd be stuck, never able to go anywhere without someone taking her.

"There's a motor scooter in the garage," Josey said. "If we can get it running, you can use it."

She pictured herself dashing about on a scooter and almost smiled. Actually, she'd been surprised when Charles hadn't demanded she return the Jeep immediately.

Her mother's hand covered hers. "Honey, I've got some money saved, but it's for school. I can't let you spend it on a car."

"I'm not calling him Dad anymore," she said, her voice quavering.

"It doesn't matter what you call him," her mother told her gently.

Josey put in, "The most stupid thing I did was not get a degree. It would give me the wherewithal to live while I paint or, in Annie's case, while she writes."

She hadn't written in the notebook since that brief, initial spurt. If she were a real writer, she'd be writing all the time.

"Is that what you want to do?" her mother asked.

"I guess," she said sullenly.

From the restaurant Josey drove to the Mill, where she introduced Liz to Mary. Annie hung in the background, browsing a little.

"Come on in the studio, Lizzie? I'll show you what I'm working on," Josey said.

When Annie started to follow, Mary smiled and took her arm. "Annie, I need your opinion on something."

"What?" She saw Josey close the studio door.

"What do you think about the arrangement here?"

Puzzled, Annie looked around. "It looks fine to me. I should go to the hardware and get the paint."

"I'll let your mother and aunt know where you are," Mary said.

As she went out the door, she distinctly heard anguish in her mother's raised voice. She paused, but Mary's pat on the back felt more like a gentle shove. Crossing the street, her thoughts turned toward Molly. Anticipation made her jittery. The overhead bell jangled as she opened the door.

One of Molly's friends, Candy, turned her head as she approached the hardware store counter, "Well, look who's here. Molly thought maybe you'd left town, Annie."

"Why would I do that?" she asked with a sense of dread. Had Molly hinted about their afternoon in bed? Somehow blamed it on Annie? She knew her face was flushed.

"We haven't seen you at the Gray Fox lately."

Annie dared a look at Molly, saw her face suffused with color, her gaze hard on Candy as if to say, *Shutup*.

"My mom's visiting this weekend." She put the empty gallon on the counter and turned away from Molly's gaze. "I need three more."

"I could bring them out to you, you know, if you called ahead of time," Molly said almost angrily. "No charge if I'm delivering anyway."

Annie's eyes briefly lit on Molly's face. "Next time maybe. I'm here now." She hoped she sounded uncaring.

Molly gave a short laugh. "I'd be doing you a favor."

"I didn't ask for one," Annie said mildly, turning to Candy. "So, anything exciting happen at the Gray Fox?"

Candy lifted plucked eyebrows. "A raid. We flew out of there like a bunch of quail scattering."

"Anybody arrested?" Luckily she hadn't been one of them.

"Some of the lake people, including Molly's Cass. They don't know Bernie. We spotted him immediately."

"He's not my Cass," Molly said.

"Who's Bernie?" Annie asked, glad to hear Molly's denial but still ignoring her.

"Police chief," Molly said. "He likes to drive his own SUV, then slap a light on the top. Sneaky. Only we're onto him."

"How come you didn't warn Cass?" Candy asked, tossing her damp hair out of her eyes. "You need some air conditioning in here."

"He told me he was twenty-one. And Dad likes to keep the back door open."

"Today I'm legal," Annie said almost to herself.

"Yeah? Happy birthday." Candy smiled. "Need some help carrying those? I'm going anyway now. See ya, Molly."

"I could have carried them," Molly said. "Happy birthday, Annie."

"Thanks. We can manage." Annie heard the sulk in Molly's voice.

Then they were out the door and loading the cans into Candy's vehicle, a bright red Mustang with the top down. "Did you walk?"

"From the Mill. Your dad lets you drive this?" Annie asked admiringly.

"Once in a while, he does." Candy gave her a faint, self-satisfied smile and a wink that startled her.

"Are you lucky!"

"Yeah. There are perks to being the bank president's daughter." Candy revved the engine and pulled out, pinning Annie to the back of the seat.

Annie laughed. "Whoa, wild woman."

They sped down the block to the Mill, the tires protesting the left turn Candy made into the parking lot. Sand flew up and settled on them as she stopped the car. "Well, shit," Candy said. "Your aunt and Durban ought to pave this."

Annie transferred the paint to the Escort. She ran a hand over the top of the Mustang's door. "Thanks for the thrill. You always drive like that?"

"Only when my dad can't see me." Candy laughed. "Got to go before I'm spotted by someone who knows him. See you." And she was gone.

Annie spit sand out of her mouth and wiped her eyes and wondered about the wink. The thought that Molly might have confided in Candy made her nervous.

She went into the Mill where her mother and aunt and Mary hung around the counter, drinking coffee and talking. The conversation stopped when they saw her, as if they had some big secret she wasn't supposed to know. It made her feel like a kid.

"We can go now," Josey said.

On the way home, Annie sensed a subtle difference in the way her mother was treating Josey, a carefulness that hadn't been there before. Annie thought of Josey as self-reliant, needing no one. She owned her own house, she was self-employed, she depended on no one, certainly no man. It made her nervous and a little surly to know she was being left out.

A tension rose from the three of them as they neared the homestead, as if each of them harbored a fear that Charles might be there. Annie hoped that he'd already come and gone if he was coming at all. She hadn't realized till then how much she dreaded seeing him again.

She spotted her stepfather's car as soon as they turned into the driveway, the Buick Riviera he washed and waxed regularly, caring more for it than his kids or his wife. Her mother gave a little gasp, and Josey cursed. "Goddamn him, can't he leave you alone for two lousy days."

"Aw, Mom," Annie protested, feeling as if she might throw up.

Jeanne ran toward them across the yard and stopped short. "Dad's on the porch. He was hot."

"This is your aunt," their mother said, standing in the sun, squinting toward the house. Like Annie, Jeanne had not seen her aunt since her grandparents' funeral.

"Call me Josey," Josey said. "You look like a Duprey."

"Do I? You look like Mom." Jeanne smiled nervously. "Happy birthday, Annie."

Annie grinned. "Come on, Jeanne. I'll show you my room. It's about twice the size of the one at home." She led her sister to the door that opened to the mud room and kitchen. "Can you stay overnight? Drive the Jeep home tomorrow?" That's why Charles had brought Jeanne, of course. He needed another driver.

"I told Dad I didn't want the Jeep, Annie." Jeanne stopped in the kitchen and stared at Josey's paintings. "Those are hers?"

"Yep."

Jeanne glanced around. Annie knew she was thinking the place looked old, rundown. "Guess she doesn't care much about the house."

Annie reacted defensively. "She doesn't have the money to fix it up. I like the place. It has character." Roy had said that.

Jeanne shrugged. "It's kind of dreary, though. All this old stuff." She saw her bedroom through Jeanne's eyes: the old furniture, the closet hidden by a curtain. "This is where Mom grew up, isn't it? Looks like nothing's changed since then."

Annie sat on the bed. "What's happening at home?"

Flopping next to her, Jeanne said, "Same old, same old. Dad's an asshole. Mom tries to keep the peace. You're lucky to be out of there."

But it was one thing to leave on her own, another altogether to be kicked out. "I don't have a home anymore."

"I'm leaving the house as soon as I can, and I bet Holly and Lisa will too."

"They okay? Holly and Lisa?" Their younger sisters, the twins.

"I guess. I don't have anyone to talk to now that you're gone. They stick together."

"Annie, Jeanne," Their mother called and shortly after appeared at the bedroom door. "It's like coming home again," she said. "Your dad's leaving."

Jeanne got up. "Do I have to go?"

Their mother shook her head. "No, sweetie, you can stay the night if you want."

"He won't be mad?" Jeanne asked.

"He said you could. I'm going to look around a bit." And she was gone.

"I'll show you the pond," Annie said. "It's neat."

XI
Josey

After the girls got back from the pond, the four of them took a look at the motorscooter. Although covered by a tarp, it looked neglected. The tires were soft, the paint dull, the chrome handlebars dotted with rust.

She hooked the battery to a charger, checked the oil, added some gas, and turned the key. Nothing. She stepped back from the scooter, aware they were not going to make the engine turn over.

"Is there anyplace around here that'll fix it?" Liz asked.

"Pulaski's maybe." The gas station in Clover. "They work on cars."

"I'll pay. Call, though, if it's going to be over a hundred." Liz looked at Josey and shrugged helplessly.

Josey knew the feeling. She nodded. "Guess we better do something we know how to do."

Liz baked a cake, then made potato salad while Josey fried hamburgers, Annie's choices for her birthday dinner. Jeanne set the table, while Annie picked salad greens.

Before dessert, Annie opened her gifts. Her sisters gave her a cotton sweater, white with a V neck. Annie put it on despite the heat. Next she opened Josey's gift, a framed painting of a great blue heron on the edge of the pond, one leg drawn up underneath it. Annie had admired the work last week. Liz gave her daughter money and then apologized.

"I always need money, Mom. Thanks." She gave her mother and sister a hug, then stood uncertainly next to Josey before giving her a loose caricature of a hug.

Josey laughed. "Am I that formidable?"

Annie flushed and Liz said, "You can be. You know it."

Later, she and Liz sat on the porch. As the twilight closed around them, the bats emerged from their roosting places and flitted silently around the yard.

"God, I didn't realize how much I missed summer nights here," Liz said, then added quietly, "Why didn't you tell me about the mastectomy?"

"I didn't want to talk about it, and I didn't want Charles to know." She figured he'd be gleeful. "I don't want him to ever know, and I don't intend to tell Annie. Promise you won't?"

"Of course. It hurts, though, your not telling me, your not trusting me."

She glanced at Liz. "It hurts to be so alienated from you."

Liz sighed and took her hand. "The painting is wonderful. You're very good at what you do."

"Thank you for that."

The girls joined them on the porch, then went on up to Annie's room, while the women sat in the soft dusk. Josey felt she never got enough of these warm evenings, that she never would. Sometimes in mid-winter, when the heat came on, she shut her eyes and pretended that the warm air was that of a summer night.

Liz and Jeanne left the next morning before noon when rain threatened. The Jeep offered no protection from the elements. Annie and Josey stood in the yard until the sound of the two vehicles was gone.

"I'm going to the Mill and give Mary a break," Josey said.

A few drops spattered from the overcast sky, and Annie looked upward. "Guess I won't paint."

Rain streaked across the windshield on the way into town. Josey closed the windows. The fan blew stale hot air around, and she was glad to step out of the car and dash into the building.

Mary looked up from the counter where she was talking to a bleached blond, the only other person in the gallery. "Your sister's gone already?"

The blond turned and became Shelley. "Is Liz gone? I didn't have time to really talk to her."

"She left this morning, just before the rain. I felt I hardly got to talk to her myself," Josey said, approaching the two women. "Everything okay, Shelley? You sounded a little upset Saturday."

"I was. Tom didn't come home Friday. It's not the first time he's stayed out all night. Said he was working on the town's equipment."

Who was she to doubt Tom Barnes? "That makes sense."

Shelley made a sound like Monty did when clearing his nose. "I'm not keeping house for him anymore. He can live at the city garage."

"Maybe you should move out. Let them all fend for themselves," Mary suggested. "They'd learn to appreciate you."

"Where would I go?"

"You could move in with me." Mary arched one eyebrow. "I'm a single woman now."

"Maybe he really was working on the equipment," Josey said.

"I'd rather think he was doing what he said he was, but it's getting so that I can't anymore." Shelley's tired smile didn't reach her eyes. "Well, I gotta get some work done at home."

Josey and Mary watched her go. The rain drummed a steady beat on the metal roof. Josey looked out the windows at the pond, steaming in the onslaught from the skies, and hoped Liz and Jeanne had driven out of it. No rain was predicted farther south. "Sell anything?" "Yep. Your painting of the Mill and some pottery. I've got a name and address here from someone who wants to commission a painting of the stream going over the dam with cedar waxwings snapping at insects. Interested?" Again Mary's eyebrow veed upward.

"Better than a portrait. I've been wanting to paint that myself."

"How was your visit with your sister?"

She bit her lower lip. "Fine. I miss her. Her bastard of a husband showed up with Annie's younger sister and took the Jeep. Liz and Jeanne stayed overnight, though."

"Husbands," Mary spat.

"You can't compare Charles to Roy. Charles is emotionally and verbally abusive. Roy always treated you like a queen."

"The only problem was he really wanted a king."

Exasperated, Josey said, "I give up."

Mary shot her a steely glance. "It's one of those no-win situations. I need to get on with things."

"Maybe we should go out for dinner and hit the bars after."

"I'm not looking for someone, Josey, certainly not someone I'd find in a bar. We can go out for dinner, though. Maybe Shelley and Ellen would go with us, and Helen if she's here."

Helen's name gave her an unpleasant jolt. She supposed Ellen was bedding her. The few times she'd made love with Ellen came back to her. She felt a touch of sorrow for something lost.

Pulling a chair up to the painting of Monty, she began adding color to his head. He looked at her out of unblinking, mahogany eyes. She wanted to finish the painting by the end of the week, which was the end of the month. Bills.

When they closed that afternoon, the rain still fell. She jumped over puddles to get to her car. At home, she ran to the house with a newspaper over her head.

Annie was sitting at the kitchen table under the bug-filled globe that lit the room. The girl looked up and smiled. "I hung the great blue heron in my room. Someday it'll be worth a lot of money, but I'll never sell it."

Josey laughed. "You're an optimist if you think I'm going to be famous someday. Did your mom and sister get home okay?"

"Yep. Mom called. They barely got rained on," Annie said. "Dinner is in the oven."

She went upstairs, the dog bounding in front of her. Putting on dry clothes, she looked at the bed longingly. She lay down for a moment, so tired that her body felt as if it had taken a beating. Yet her mind roamed endlessly, skimming over the day's events, never lighting onto one thing very long.

She placed a hand on the left side of her chest, still unable to accept the numbness, the loss. The scar looked and felt like a piece of cardboard left out in the rain and dried in the sun. She'd seen the muscle moving under the skin. It reminded her of a stump after amputation.

The smell of roasting meat drifted up the stairs. She dragged herself upright and went downstairs. Food that smelled so good would surely revive her.

Annie had just pulled a small, charred roast out of the oven. She was mashing potatoes.

"Need some help?" Josey said.

"You can make a salad and cut the bread," Annie said. "Sorry about the roast. I didn't know how long to leave it in."

"Hey, I'm not complaining. Any time you want to cook, you've got my gratitude."

After dinner, she and Annie sat on the porch, hemmed in by the rain. Josey longed for a cigarette. Although she knew Annie was aware that she smoked, she felt too uncomfortable to light up in front of her. When a breeze kicked up and sent snatches of rain their way, Josey went to bed.

Sometime in the night the rain ceased and the sky cleared. Josey awakened around three to see the stars outside her windows. At five, she arose and showered, then left for the Mill.

She worked on the *Woman In Blue*, adding black to the blue for dimension, for shadows. Standing back to study it, she felt keenly the loss of purpose that accompanied every finished work of hers. Especially this one.

Closing the studio door, she locked the front door behind her and walked to Pulaski's. The rain had cleared the humidity from the air, cooling it, and she hurried to keep warm.

"Hey, Sam," she said to Pulaski who was behind the counter, "You're just the one I want to see." He was a big man, who had played football with Tom Barnes. She thought they were still good friends. His hands rested on the glass countertop, the seams and fingernails embedded with grease and oil.

"Hey yourself, Josey. What's up?"

She told him about the scooter.

"I'll send someone out to look at it. Maybe they can fix it there. Otherwise, we'll load it up and bring it in. Want the oil changed, too?"

"It needs to be done." She could do that, she thought, but she didn't want to.

She walked to the coffee shop next. Scanning the room for an empty table, she spotted Ellen waving at her and took a chair across from her. "Busy place."

"I was hoping someone would show up. I hate eating alone." Ellen looked at her out of eyes so clear and blue that Josey felt a twinge of envy. Ellen slept well.

Shelley hurried over to fill their cups. "Morning, girls. When you're ready to order, holler."

Sipping at the hot brew, Josey eyed Ellen through the steam. "Caffeine is what I need right now."

"I brought lunch," Ellen said, her gaze steady.

"You did that last week," Josey remarked.

"Well, it's the only way I see you these days."

Josey dropped her voice. "Why you want to see me at all is the question."

"The real question is why can't we be friends." Ellen cocked her head. A quiver at one end of her smile gave away her nervousness.

Josey had no good answer. She looked away. "How was your weekend with Helen?"

"We spent Saturday on the river. She fished, I read. That was nice." Ellen opened the menu. "How was yours?"

"Good. It's always wonderful to see my sister."

"You must have stayed up late talking. You look tired."

"I am. I don't sleep well. Like Shelley here."

Shelley was standing next to the table, ready to take their orders. "What'll it be, girls?"

XII
Annie

She leaned against the ladder, high up, pleased and excited. Molly had just slammed the door of the delivery pickup and was walking across the wet grass toward Annie.

"Hi. I was out this way and decided to stop and see how far you'd gotten."

"I don't need any paint yet."

Molly stood at the base of the ladder, hands in her back pockets, looking up at her. "Well, are you coming down?"

Annie kept slapping the paint on the bare boards. "When the brush is dry."

"I'm not standing here and yelling at you. I've got to get back to the store in an hour."

Annie climbed down the ladder, carrying the can with her. She hammered the lid shut, put the brush in a plastic bag, and fastened it with a twist tie. "There." She glanced at her paint-speckled watch. It was noon. "Are you hungry?"

Molly shrugged. "I guess."

"Come on inside. You look cold." Molly wore shorts and a sleeveless pullover.

"I am."

In the kitchen, with a hammering heart belying her calm exterior, Annie asked, "Do you want lunch before or after?" There was lust in Molly's eyes, she was sure.

"After." The thickness of the word telltale.

Upstairs, she felt emboldened. Never taking her eyes off Molly's, she undressed her and tossed her clothing on the one chair in the room. She let her own fall on the floor.

Molly's eyes became slits, her smile a crooked gleam. She seized Annie by the shoulders, pushed her onto the bed, and fell on top of her.

Pinned, Annie struggled to roll Molly over. When Molly began kissing her, she gave up. She came almost as soon as Molly touched her.

Raising herself on an elbow, she looked at the small, firm breasts, the flat, firm belly. She tested the wet mat with her fingers. Molly moaned a little, took hold of Annie's head, and pushed it downward.

Thrilled and a little shocked by the audacity, Annie sandwiched herself between Molly's legs, her neck at an awkward angle.

After, Molly looked at her watch and got to her feet. She turned her back to pull on her clothes. "Gotta go. Dad's gonna kill me."

"What about lunch?" Annie asked, dressing.

"No time. Look, don't take this too seriously," Molly said, face flushed, eyes darting away. "It's a safe and sure quickie."

Although her legs still trembled, Annie nodded. "Same here."

She washed up after Molly sped out of the yard. Ravenous and dreamy with remembered lust, she fixed herself a sandwich and ate it on the porch.

Later, she thought that might have been why she fell off the ladder, twisting her ankle on landing. Crying out with pain, unable to get up at first, she managed to pull herself to her feet using the ladder as a prop. Sure she was being punished, she hopped toward the house, the pain pounding through her veins and arteries.

John Lovelace drove in, jumped out of his Bronco, and loped in her direction. "Hey, girl, what happened?"

Annie let him help her into the house. He sat her in a chair, propping her ankle on another, while he bagged ice out of the freezer. "The paint and the brush . . ." she said.

"I'll get them as soon as I'm done here."

"What good will I be now? I can't climb a ladder like this." She fought tears. She couldn't make love either.

"Maybe you'll be all right in a week or two," he said.

"A week or two," she said with dismay, swabbing at her eyes with the heel of her hand. "Damn."

"I'm going out to take care of the paint and stuff. Then maybe we should go get an X-ray."

"Can't," she said. "No insurance." That had ended with her suspension.

When he came back, he brought a pressure bandage to wrap her ankle in, then fastened the ice around it with a towel. "There," he said with a satisfied smile. "Dr. Lovelace at your service. I always carry one of those with me. You never know when you have to wrap a horse. It smells a little like one, too."

Her pleasure punctured, she barely managed to thank him.

"Hey, I wondered where you'd gone to. That's why I stopped. I'm off to a horse show again tomorrow. Wanted to say goodbye." He peered at her. "Cheer up. It could be a broken leg or a broken head, both of which I've had, thanks to horses."

She sniffed. All she wanted was for him to leave her alone in her misery so that she could take a shower. "I'll be okay now, John."

"I'm not going anywhere until someone comes home." He sat across the table from her.

"I want to take a shower," she said.

"I'll help you get there and wait outside the door, but I'm not leaving."

When Josey came home, she'd fallen asleep on top of her rumpled sheets.

"How'd this happen?" Josey stood at the end of the bed, frowning.

She'd wakened when her aunt walked into the room. "I fell off the ladder. John helped me get inside. He wrapped the ankle and put ice on it."

"Nice boy, John Lovelace. He got a thing for you?"

She gestured at her ankle and began to sob. "I can't paint." But that wasn't why she was crying.

"The painting can wait. I'm going to fix something to eat. Want a tray?"

"I want to go downstairs." The throbbing in her ankle, when upright, made her more determined. She had to get over this, quick.

Once Josey got her down the stairs, Annie hopped to the table and sat. She picked up her damaged leg and propped it on another chair.

Josey emptied the ice bag and refilled it, wrapping the towel around the Ace bandage. "We should get this X-rayed."

Shaking her head, Annie said she couldn't afford to pay for it herself. When Josey headed toward the phone, Annie stopped her. "Don't call Mom. It'll get better on its own."

"Well, if it's not better in a few days, we're going whether you like it or not."

Annie slumped in her chair. "I'll be on it in a few days." She apologized, sensing her aunt's annoyance.

Josey said, "I'm not upset with you. I took the horse portrait out to Lovelaces', and he said he didn't like it enough to pay five hundred."

"It's gorgeous." Annie was momentarily roused from her self-pity. "How could he say that?"

"Thanks, but it's a sorry fact that some people get down and dirty when it comes to money. He's one of them. I think his wife will change his mind, though." Josey looked less glum. "Why was John here?"

"He stopped by to say hello. I was hopping to the house."

Brenda called while they were eating. "All right. I'll bring it by tomorrow after work. Thanks, Brenda." Josey winked at Annie.

Annie's ankle pulsed with pain. She wanted a book to read to take her mind off it. She even thought about watching TV. Since she'd been here, no one had turned the television on. She wasn't sure it worked. At home, it was never off when Charles was around.

When Josey was done with the dishes, she turned to Annie. "Where do you want to be, Annie? Upstairs, downstairs, on the porch?"

When Annie didn't know and could only sulk, Josey left her alone.

The next morning, Josey helped Annie downstairs before leaving. She hopped moodily from one room to the other. Flipping on the TV, which tuned in a few stations, she watched the morning shows for a while. Bored with that, she went through the bookcases and came up with another novel. Hopping to the porch with her bag of ice and the book, she sat down, tied the ice around her ankle with the towel, and lifted her leg to the railing.

When she'd put her foot on the floor that morning, the almost unbearable pain had dulled to a throb after a few moments. She thought in a few days she'd be able to limp around. Maybe by next week she'd be back on the ladder.

The morning passed slowly. Half hoping Molly would turn up but knowing how frustrating or painful that might prove to be, she was only slightly disappointed when she didn't show. It would be nice to have someone to talk to, she was thinking when she made a sandwich around one.

"Brought you something," Josey said from the door.

She hadn't heard her aunt come in and almost put her foot down in surprise.

Josey held out a pair of crutches. "Try them on for size. They're about right for me. I rented them at the clinic."

"Thanks." She nestled them under her arms and swung between them a few steps. It wasn't as easy as it looked.

"They said you should be X-rayed," Josey said.

"It's just a sprain," she insisted, although the chance that it might be more worried her.

"I talked to your mom. She said to X-ray it. She'll pay."

At that she caved in, muttering, "I feel like a kid."

She clamped her lips against crying out when the technician positioned her ankle at different angles. The X-rays showed no fractures. She was a ball of sweat, limp with relief.

Josey filled the Tylenol with codeine prescription at the clinic pharmacy before driving her home. "Well, you were right. Still, it's better to know."

Annie was looking out the car window at the flowers blooming. She had taken a pill before leaving the clinic and was already sleepy. Her eyes closed.

"Looks like Menken's truck," her aunt said, and Annie's lids flew open.

"Sometimes she stops when she's out this way." Molly was leaning against the side of the pickup, arms and legs crossed. Looking sexy.

"You're good friends?" Josey parked next to the pickup.

"Yeah. Good friends," she agreed, feeling slightly loopy. Marijuana and codeine did that to her.

"Hi, Molly," Josey said, getting out of the Escort. "Maybe you can help me with the patient here."

But Annie waved them away. Steadying herself with the crutches, she swung toward the house.

"I'll get her to bed," Molly offered, "if you have to get back to work."

"Don't you?" Josey asked.

"Not for a while," Molly said, catching up with Annie.

"Okay," Josey said. "I'll be home after I go to Lovelaces', Annie."

Annie focused on the house, willing herself to get there. Molly opened the doors for her. She knew she'd have to go to bed. The question was how would she get there. At the base of the stairs, she stopped.

"I can crawl up them," she said, "or you can take some of my weight."

"Anything to get you in bed." Molly grinned. "Just kidding."

Once there, though, Annie felt herself being drawn into a sleep she couldn't ignore, not even for Molly.

XIII
Josey

It was damn cold for the end of June, Josey thought. She shivered in a northerly wind. Brenda Lovelace was hurrying out of the house, pulling on a denim jacket. Bud was coming out of the barn, the doberman at his side.

The horse trailer and pickup were gone from their spot beside the stable. John must be somewhere with a horse or two.

"Come on inside," Brenda said. "Put Macho in the barn, Bud."

The doberman silently circled the Escort, eyeing Buddy hungrily. Feeling safe behind the closed windows, Buddy gnashed his teeth against the glass. Putting huge paws on the door, the doberman peered inside. Buddy dropped out of sight.

Bud laughed. "Your dog's got some smarts anyway. He knows when to back off."

Josey bit off a retort, saying instead, "Let me get the painting out of the back." She carried it inside, turning an edge into the cutting wind. Brenda opened doors for her.

She set the painting on the long leather couch, facing a huge stone fireplace. It was supposed to hang over a mantel already covered with horse trophies. Looking around, she saw that every available surface carried at least one trophy.

Brenda backed away a few feet and Josey uncovered the portrait for her to see. "It's wonderful," Brenda exclaimed, clasping her hands together. "He looks alive. I love it."

Bud walked in on stocking feet and stood next to his wife with his arms crossed. "Can't blame a guy for trying to deal."

Asshole, Josey thought. She said nothing while Brenda wrote a check for six hundred, the price they'd agreed on for the portrait and the photos. "Thanks, Brenda," she said on her way out the door. Both of the Lovelaces headed toward the barn.

"I'll spread the word," Brenda called, "and get you some more business."

And I'll have contracts next time, she promised herself.

The following morning she stopped at the grocery store and bought bagels, cream cheese, and a macaroni salad at the deli counter. There was nothing to make sandwiches with at home except the peanut butter and jam that Annie devoured every day. It was Josey's turn to bring the lunch that was turning into a daily event.

She let herself in the Mill and locked the door behind her. Seven-fifteen was late. Mary was already there, working. Josey's painting was gone.

"Where is it?" Her first thought, an irrational one, was that someone had broken in and stolen it.

"On the wall in the other room. Go look." Mary wiped her hands on a dirty towel and trailed after her.

The morning light streamed in the wall of windows overlooking the mill pond and focused on the *Woman in Blue*. Josey's breath caught in her throat. "When did you hang it?"

"This morning. It's finished, Josey. You said so yourself. It's too good to hide."

She walked over to the wall and lifted it from the hanger. "I'm not ready. It's going to be one in a series anyway." Carrying it back to the studio, she set it on the easel and covered it.

Mary followed her. "What are you afraid of, Josey? Why would anyone think it was you in the painting?"

"It's my painting, my choice." She felt anger at what she considered a presumptuous act.

"All right. I shouldn't have hung it without asking. You're afraid Ellen will guess, aren't you?"

She poured herself a cup of coffee and put lunch in the old fridge before answering. "People will want to know where the idea came from."

"Tell a white lie." Mary's dark eyes held her gaze.

She didn't look away. "I'm not going to do that."

"Okay. I give up."

"I appreciate your support, Mary. I know it doesn't seem that way, but I do."

Mary gave her a squeeze. "You'll always have it."

"Thanks." She smiled. "Time to work."

She began another sketch of the woman in the mirror, this one with both breasts. Josey intended the painting to convey the impending loss that the *Woman in Blue* portrayed. She had yet to decide on a color.

Mary turned on public radio. The soothing voices and the classical music became background sound to Josey's concentration. She barely noticed Mary, pausing while glazing.

"This is the *Woman in Blue* before the mastectomy?" Mary asked.

"Yep." She momentarily lost her concentration.

"It's time to open," Mary said. "You keep working. I'll go."

When it was noon, Mary called her to lunch. She heard the familiar murmur of Ellen's voice and quickly covered the sketch before putting the bagels in the microwave to nuke. She felt ebullient, pleased with what she'd accomplished that morning.

"We're having a local artists' exhibit at the library. We have a glass case for the pottery. The paintings, of course, will go on the wall. Would you two be interested?" Ellen asked.

Mary jumped at the chance. "How many pieces do you want?"

The open neck of Ellen's blouse drew Josey's gaze. There was no perspiration trapped in the cleavage today. She'd always been attracted to breasts, to the aesthetics of curves.

Ellen caught her looking. Her color deepened, but she kept talking. "As many as we can exhibit. We won't be selling them. Under your names we'll put the Pottery and Art Mill. If somebody wants to purchase anything, we'll point them your way."

Josey swallowed the piece of bagel she was chewing. "When do you want the stuff?"

"How about tomorrow after work? We can catch a bite to eat in town and set up the exhibit afterwards."

"Sounds good to me," Mary said. "Josey?"

"Sure." She took a forkful of macaroni and let it slide down her throat. Tactilely, eating was like sex, she thought, the sensations similar.

After Ellen left, Mary said, "That case won't hold more than five pieces, and I don't want my stuff sitting around for someone to break."

Josey walked around the room, looking at her paintings on the wall. "What do you think? A few of these or should I recycle some of the ones stacked in the back room?"

"Nice of Ellen to promote our art, don't you think?" Mary said.

"I think Ellen's a little like a spider weaving a web. I can't get away from her."

"Isn't that a bit egotistical, considering she has Helen?" Mary's eyebrow veed.

Josey tried to shrug off the stinging truth. When two women came through the door, effectively shutting off the dialogue, she went into the back room.

There she looked through her paintings stacked along the walls. She'd take some of these over, she thought, setting aside a few favorites. Done, she took over the counter. "Go ahead, Mary. Do your thing."

She studied the women as they rounded the room. They were lookers, not buyers, she decided. One of them turned and asked her if she was the one who painted portraits.

"Did you paint Monty, Lovelaces' horse?" The woman was bedecked with silver jewelry.

"Yes," she said, wary of anyone associated with Bud Lovelace.

The woman turned to her friend. "It's over their fireplace."

"I've seen it," the friend replied. "It's very good."

"We have a mare my daughter shows. Do you do people on their horses?"

"Sure," she said. "It costs a little more."

The woman waved a hand in the air as if money was no matter. The bracelets made a tinkling sound. "Come out and see the horse and my daughter and give me a price."

"Okay," Josey said. "Write down your name and address. I'll come tonight if it's okay." She could hand-write a contract.

When the women left, she opened a book that lay on the shelf under the counter.

She hadn't been aware there were so many horse farms in the area. The stable wasn't as impressive as Lovelaces', but the house was immense with an inground pool in the backyard. She parked in front of the garage.

The woman, Maureen Brewster, told Josey to call her Reenie. She introduced Josey to her daughter, Candy, who was a slender, athletic version of her mother.

Candy said, "I know your niece, Annie."

Josey put the names together. These were the wife and the daughter of George Brewster, the president of the bank in town. She'd seen the girl zipping around in a red Mustang convertible.

"What did you have in mind?" she asked.

"A portrait of Candy on her horse. Brenda said you take photos and use them as models."

"I've got my camera," she said, gesturing at the car. A miniature schnauzer stood barking at Buddy through the closed window. The schnauzer's snout was brown with something it had eaten, and bits of hay and sawdust clung to its coat.

"Hush, you silly thing." Reenie picked up the dirty little animal. Thinking of the doberman, Josey liked these people better for their choice of dogs.

"Get your show clothes on, Candy," Reenie said before turning to Josey. "We cleaned up the mare after we got home. It won't take long to saddle her."

"That's okay. We've still got good light."

Candy came out dressed in a long-sleeved, checked shirt tucked into jeans, belted with leather and fastened by a huge silver buckle. Over the jeans she wore smooth leather chaps with silver conchos. The girl's hair was neatly pulled back under a cowboy hat that completed the outfit. She was transformed from an ordinary kid into someone glamorous.

Josey stood outside the stable with Reenie and made small talk while Candy saddled the horse and led her out of the barn. She mounted in one fluid movement.

The dark chestnut mare had three white socks and a thin strip of white down her nose. She blew her nostrils clean. Josey stepped backwards out of the spray. Then the horse shook and particles of dust flew from her shiny coat.

Candy laughed. "Cut it out, Snippers. She always does this when we're lined up in front of the judge. It's so embarrassing."

Josey snapped photos of Candy and Snippers against different backgrounds. It was more difficult with the girl. She had to back up to get the two of them in focus. In order to hone in on details, she took separate close-ups of the girl and the horse under her.

When Candy rolled up her chaps and walked the mare to the barn, Josey put away the camera and brought out the contract she'd written. "Six hundred, including photos."

"I thought you said it'd be more expensive than Monty's portrait." Reenie cocked a thin eyebrow.

"It's enough," Josey said with a slight grin. "I'll call you when the photos are developed." She lowered herself into the Escort, pushing Buddy off her seat.

The little dog in Reenie's arms struggled to get down, and Reenie hugged him to her. "Not yet, Cuddles."

Josey nearly laughed. Reenie looked like someone who would name her dog Cuddles, just as Bud Lovelace had fittingly named his dog Macho.

The weather warmed during the night and Josey awakened in a sweat. She left the house as colors streaked the clouds and birdsong broke the before-dawn hush. She felt most at peace in the early mornings when the day was full of possibilities. Then she forgot her loss and her fears.

When she reached the Mill, quiet except for the hum of the fridge and the ticking of the clock over the door, she transferred her worries to canvas. The phone rang, and she snatched it up when she could no longer ignore the sound.

"I saw your car and the lights," Ellen said in her ear. "Open up. I want to talk to you."

"Where are you?"

"Outside on the porch."

She covered her canvas before unlocking the door and swinging it open.

Ellen held up a cell phone. "Handy little things."

"We'll see each other at noon, won't we?"

"I want to talk to you alone." Ellen wore another blouse open to the second button. Josey's quick glance in that direction apparently did not go unnoticed. "For one thing, why do you keep looking at me like that if you're not interested?"

Josey cleared her throat and said the first thing that came to mind. "I'm an artist. I like breasts. I like curves."

Ellen said quietly, "Oh."

Josey took a step back and crossed her arms. "May I ask how Helen fits in your life?"

"I need an old friend right now, and she's that." Ellen's smile trembled a little at the edges. "I don't understand you."

Josey studied her for a moment. Maybe it was the vulnerability that decided for her—the brave, lopsided grin. Perhaps it was what Ellen refrained from saying. She ran her tongue over her lips. "Want to see what I'm working on?"

She led Ellen into the studio, realizing she'd never invited her there till now. The track lights glared even in the daylight that crept into the room. She whipped the covers off the paintings, keeping her eyes on Ellen's face.

For a long moment Ellen stared at them, a puzzled look coming and going. She cleared her throat, her voice unsteady. "Powerful." Her eyes strayed to Josey's face and back to the easels. "You're telling me something here? This is you." The last sentence had no question in it. Ellen had put it together.

Josey nodded, frowning at the canvases. "I don't want to talk about it, though."

"When you do, let me know. I'll listen." Ellen added wistfully, "I wish you'd trusted me, though."

"I didn't want anyone to know," Josey said.

"Obviously. It's nevertheless quite a jolt to find out you felt you had to hide it from me. Puts things pretty much in perspective."

"I didn't want any pity," she explained, feeling somewhat at a loss as to why she'd expected any.

"You wouldn't have gotten any from me. I'll go now." Ellen briefly pressed her eyes shut with a thumb and forefinger.

Josey said softly, "I couldn't talk about it. It was a shock."

Ellen nodded, dropping her hand to her side. "I'll bet. I'm sorry."

Josey turned away. She heard the door shut behind Ellen.

XIV
Annie

The week passed slowly. She read, wrote in the notebook, and put more weight on her ankle. Nearly every day Molly drove in for a quick bout in bed, always saying before leaving that it meant nothing.

Josey asked who was stopping by. "I see the tire tracks in the sand. They're not mine."

"Sometimes John, sometimes Molly. You'd make a good spy." She was damn lonely, hungering for someone to talk to, but she wouldn't admit to it.

"Tell you what. Tomorrow night we'll go for a ride on the scooter," Josey said. Pulaski had dropped the scooter off after Annie sprained her ankle "Take it into town and get some ice cream."

She smiled a little. "I haven't been away from here since this happened, but maybe we should go in the Escort. What if we fall over?"

"You don't trust me, I see. That was my scooter first. I rode it everywhere, but we can take the car. Then Buddy can come along. He loves ice cream."

John called her on Friday. She heard Macho's deep bark in the background.

"Where are you?" she asked.

"In the barn. Is your ankle good enough to go to the Fox?"

"You bet," she said, jumping at the chance to get out. "I've got cabin fever." It had been one of the longest weeks of her life, coming in second to the two days she and her sisters had been left with their dad when her mother had gone to a convention in Madison a few years ago.

"Nine okay?"

"Sure." She pictured the inside of the stable, the dog patrolling the aisles, a horse in the cross-ties. "How was the show?"

"Good. I'll tell you more tonight."

She used the bannister to hop upstairs to take a shower and wash her hair. Josey had rented a chair to put in the tub for her to sit on, and she enjoyed the warm spray for a long time before turning it off.

Molly had come and gone around noon time, saying nothing about her weekend plans, and Annie hadn't asked. The sex was so good now that she knew she would never voluntarily give it up, nor did she think Molly would. Perhaps her showing up at the Fox with John would make Molly a little jealous. She, too, could pretend the only reason to have sex with a girl was to keep her ready for when the right guy came along.

Putting her good foot outside the tub, she sat on the flat edge and dried, then levered herself over to the toilet and to the sink where she hauled herself upright. Everything took so much time and effort that it wore her out.

She was getting pretty good on the crutches and could let the foot with the bad ankle graze the ground, even take a little weight. She hoped to be able to put enough pressure on it to climb a ladder next week.

Dressed in shorts and T-shirt, throwing a cotton sweater over her shoulders, she made her way downstairs on her rump. It was less risky that way.

She heard Josey in the kitchen, talking to the dog who quickly discovered her in the hallway. "Hey, doggie," she said with a soft laugh, "Can't sneak up on you, can I?" before swinging into the kitchen.

"Look at you, all dressed up," Josey said. "Going out?"

"Yep. John called late this afternoon. He's picking me up."

Josey leaned against the counter, arms crossed, mouth straight, and Annie searched her mind for something she'd done to displease her. But it wasn't herself Josey was mad at, she concluded, it was someone or something else.

Her aunt made hamburger patties, shaping them with the heel of her hand. Opening a large can of baked beans and taking leftover potato salad out of the fridge, she put the hamburgers in a frying pan on the stove.

Annie set the table.

Dinner was a silent affair. She looked at Josey, thinking of things to say, and then said nothing. She wanted supper over. "I'll clean up."

Josey nodded, but before she left the room for outside, she squeezed Annie's shoulder.

Annie had spent her growing years living in tension, never knowing when her stepdad would blow, all of them tiptoeing around trying to please him. She hadn't even realized how awful it was until she'd left. It had taken weeks to be rid of the anxiety. It didn't take much to bring it back.

When John drove in, he stepped down from the Bronco and began talking to Josey who was cleaning out the garage that Roy had put on the foundation a week after the concrete was poured. Annie hadn't seen him since. Her aunt was tossing stuff onto the sand driveway.

She swung herself toward them, putting most of her weight on the crutches, and heard John say, "I've heard more compliments about that portrait."

"Tell your mother thanks for getting me another customer." Her aunt stood with hands on hips, her hair disheveled, a smudge of dirt on her face. She smiled. "Reenie Brewster commissioned me to paint her daughter Candy and their horse Snippers."

"Nice mare. She and Candy do well at the shows around here. They don't go out of state very often. They should."

When Annie reached them, she let her bad foot touch the ground lightly and rested.

"Hey, Annie, you'll be dancing soon," John observed, then said to Josey, "We'll leave you to your work unless you want me to stay and help."

"Go, go. Have fun. Not too much booze." Josey waved them away.

John said, "Okay to both," and opened the door of the Bronco for Annie. He winked at her as he slid behind the wheel and spoke softly. "We'll smoke dope instead, and I've got some good stuff."

"My choice of drugs is cold beer," Annie reminded him.

John backed around and drove out, waving a hand out his window. "So, how was your week?"

"Boring," she said. "And yours?"

"Okay. Why don't you go with me next week. It's a whole different world, people living and breathing horses. I sleep, cook, and pee in the trailer. There's room for two."

"Your mom would love that," she said, but she was thinking that it might make Molly sit up and take notice and maybe not say the things she did. She glanced at John, his ears pink with sunburn. He was too nice a guy to use.

"My mother doesn't need to know. Think about it. Be nice to have company."

She could tell Josey she was visiting Sue, her old college friend. Sue owed her for deserting her at that frat house party. "When, where, how long?"

"Monday, Indianapolis, back on Friday."

Four days without Molly. "No fooling around."

He raised both hands from the wheel and grinned at her. "Promise."

John opened the door at the Fox, and the smell of beer floated toward them on a billow of cigarette smoke. Annie swung inside, knowing she would soon reek of both. The crowd parted to make room for Annie's crutches.

Candy and Molly sat at the bar with Cass standing behind and Roger Kaminski sitting next to them. Candy's brows drew together at Annie's approach.

"Fell off a ladder, I hear," Candy said, "and John rescued you. A knight you are, Lovie."

"Let her sit down, Rog," John said to Roger, who was already getting up.

"I was going to." Roger took his beer and shouldered his way through the throng of young people.

Music blaring from the speakers made them shout to be heard. "Want a smoke?" Candy asked Annie.

"No, thanks. Just a cold beer."

"Your aunt's painting my horse and me," Candy said. "Mom loved the way Monty looked on canvas."

"Are you going to Indianapolis next week?" John asked.

"Nope. Too far for us."

"We are. Keep it quiet, though, will you?" John put in.

"You're going too, Annie?" Candy said.

Annie nodded.

Molly looked from Annie to John, shadows flitting across her face. She turned her head toward Cass who hovered nearby. "I need some air, Cass. Let's go outside."

There was no winning here, Annie realized, dejectedly watching her go.

∾⟊∾

John arrived Monday morning around seven. Annie had figured Josey would be gone by then. She was. John stowed Annie's bag in the living compartment of the four-horse gooseneck trailer and helped her climb into the one-ton truck.

They arrived at the Indiana State Fairgrounds late afternoon and parked near the horse barns to unload, then moved the rig to the asphalt with the many others. It became thickly hot and humid the farther south they journeyed. She made her way through a damp, heavy, invisible air curtain as she swung toward the stables. Along the way John introduced her to people whose names she immediately forgot.

After feeding and watering the horses, John unhooked the trailer and drove them to a nearby restaurant. When they returned to the fairgrounds, he rode Monty and the three-year-old mare in the outdoor arena. Dust rising from under the horses' hooves hung in a pall over the riders and observers.

The showing started the next morning. John arose before dawn to feed the two horses they'd brought. Annie heard him leave and climbed down from the huge bed over the gooseneck where she'd slept with him. As promised, he hadn't touched her.

For a while she sat in the stands at the practice arena and watched as horses and riders raised more clouds of dust. Then she crutched her way through the temporary shops that sold horse paraphernalia, everything from trucks and trailers to saddles and other tack, hats and boots, and jewelry. It fascinated her, this segment of society engaged in the showing of horses. The money spent on the horse industry astounded her. Something as small as a silver encrusted show bit for a horse's mouth sold for several hundred dollars.

The competition took place indoors, starting with halter. Annie found John before he went into his first class. They stood outside the indoor arena, sipping coffee and eating sugar donuts. He brushed off his clothes before entering the show arena. She dumped the rest of the coffees and crutched her way to a seat to watch.

Monty placed third behind two long-necked, long-legged horses that looked so much like him she wouldn't have known which should be first, but she jumped up and down a little and clapped her hands. John threw her a grin as he led the stallion out into the sunshine. The two horses in front of Monty were shown by well-known trainers, he told her. He was pleased with third.

The mare placed sixth. It was a point, John said, better than nothing. He had a little time to go through the shops with her, to eat Italian sausages on buns and fries with vinegar. Then he saddled both animals and rode them before the performance classes began.

The riding classes interested her more, and she entertained herself by picking out potential winners. The organ startled her at first. It hadn't been played during the halter classes. The music picked up the beat of the different gaits—a rollicking one for a canter, a little slower for a trot, sedate when the horses and riders were asked for a walk.

That night they were both tired. They heated up a can of baked beans and fried burgers on the little stove in the trailer, and took the food outside to eat in lawn chairs in the hot dusty night. John checked on the horses before they went to bed.

When Friday morning arrived, she was tired of the dust and heat and endless classes, and excited about going home. Leaving early in the morning, John turned into her driveway around three in the afternoon. There was no vehicle parked in front of the garage, and she felt relief. She'd gotten away with her duplicity.

She stepped out of the truck, stiff after the long drive. Every day she'd put more weight on her injured ankle. When she first stepped on it, it throbbed, forcing her to lean on the crutches until the pulsing stopped. It was like hitting the ground after her legs had been dangling too long.

John carried her bag to the house. "Hope we can do that again. Those shows get lonely."

"I'll bet."

"Want to go to the Fox tonight?" he asked, his face and ears aglow from the Indiana sun.

"I'll be ready."

Summer

XV

Josey

Josey's eyes narrowed when she saw the truck and trailer tracks in the sand, identical to the ones she'd noticed earlier in the week. She knew Annie was home. And was sure her niece had not been with her friend, although she hadn't called Sue's number. She resented what to her was unnecessary and insulting dishonesty.

Water was running when she and the dog climbed the stairs to the second floor. Buddy plunked down outside the bathroom door, his tail brushing the floor in anticipation. When Annie limped out into the hall, she let out a little yelp of surprise.

Josey came to the door of her bedroom. "How was your visit with your friend?"

"Good, fine."

"She must have a truck and trailer."

"What?"

"The tracks in the driveway."

"Oh, yeah," Annie said, flushing under her sunburn. She bent to pat the dog and tried to change the subject. "I can walk again."

"I see." Josey looked intently at her niece. "Next time, Annie, have the courtesy to tell me where you're really going and with whom." Then she retreated to her room to change before going downstairs.

In the kitchen, Annie said softly, "I'm sorry. I went to a horse show in Indianapolis with John Lovelace. He's a friend is all, and his mom didn't know." The girl met her aunt's gaze. "I am twenty-one, you know."

Josey said, "All the more reason to tell me where you're going. Why lie?"

Annie ducked her head and muttered, "I thought you'd disapprove. My stepfather would have."

"Yeah, well I'm not Charles," Josey said.

"Don't tell Mom. Okay? She'll just worry."

"I'm not about to tattle on you unless you do something dangerous to your health. Next time give me a chance."

"Okay. Sorry. I will," the girl said shamefacedly.

Josey let it go. "Are you hungry?"

"Starved," Annie said. "We ate macaroni and cheese out of a box, baked beans out of a can, stuff like that."

When dinner was over, the dishes cleaned up, and Annie gone, Josey sat on the front porch and finished off the wine. The hot breeze that had blown all day brushed her bare skin. She shook a cigarette out of the pack she left on the windowsill and lit it. "I've got to quit this," she said, inhaling.

Darkness was falling around her when Ellen drove in. Josey squashed the cigarette underfoot and put it into her pocket, then popped a stick of gum in her mouth. Ellen disliked the smell of cigarettes.

Under the bug-filled light, Ellen climbed the steps to the porch. "Sit with me," Josey said.

Ellen leaned backwards against the railing, facing Josey. "Is that why you sent me away? Because of the mastectomy?"

Josey was eye level with Ellen's cleavage. She remembered the heft of her breasts and wondered if her sexual desire was returning. Lifting her gaze, she focused on Ellen's face. "Yes. I couldn't tell you. I'm sorry. And now you have Helen." The wine had gone to her head. She'd drunk most of a bottle.

"I've always had Helen. She's my good friend, like I told you. Can you and I see each other now that I know?"

"You're gone almost every weekend," Josey pointed out, trying to hang onto the conversation. She felt at a disadvantage.

"There was no reason to stick around." Ellen looked closer at her. "You're drunk."

"I could lie down and sleep." It had been weeks since she'd slept more than four or five hours a night.

"How about a hug," Ellen suggested.

Josey said, "All right," and let herself be drawn against the softness that was Ellen. Her head reeled. "Want to come upstairs with me?"

Once there, Josey asked, "Where is Helen anyway?"

"At home." Ellen perched on the only chair in the room. "She's seeing someone."

"Really?" Her curiosity peaked. "Anyone you know?"

"I met him last time I was there. I won't be going over so often now."

"Him?" Josey asked in surprise.

"She's straight." Ellen's brows rose in exasperation. "Do I have to spell it out? Helen and I are friends."

"Is that why you're here?"

"Yes. I went to the Mill but you were already gone. So I came here."

Josey fell back on the bed. "You want to do it?"

"You have such a way with words."

"Why don't you just lie down here with me. It's too hot for sex anyway."

Ellen settled in a separate space next to Josey. "I wish every night was as warm as this one."

"Me too. I love to sweat." She was drifting off, unable to keep her eyes open or her mind focused. It felt wonderful.

When she woke up and glanced at the clock, she saw she'd only slept for half an hour. Feeling eyes on her, she turned her head and met Ellen's soft brown gaze. Her throat constricted, and she looked away. "Don't," she said hoarsely.

"Don't what?" A whisper.

"I don't want to be pitied or patronized."

"And you won't be, because I don't feel that way about you." Ellen's warm hand closed over her wrist.

"Goddamn it, Ellen, I'm too old to seduce."

"Nobody's too old." Teasing.

She rolled onto her side, the easier to see Ellen. It had been months, and during that time she'd thought she'd felt nothing, that her desire had died with the loss of the breast. She expected it to be reborn after reconstruction, but here it was welling up inside her. A surprise.

Ellen shivered but didn't move when Josey ran a hand lightly up and down her arm. She put a finger on the blood pulsing in Ellen's neck just under her skin, and murmured, "I never had this effect on anyone before."

"I never felt this way before. Pity," Ellen said.

"Why is it a pity?"

"It's a shame to waste it."

"It was the surgery." The word *cancer* stuck in her throat. "When I was a kid I had rheumatic fever, and I didn't want anyone to know about it. That's the way I felt about this."

"You told Mary." Ellen said.

Josey rolled onto her back. "Mary doesn't want me."

"You aren't making sense."

"To me, I am. Anyway, it wasn't anything you did. I haven't wanted anyone since the surgery," she said, adding quietly, "until today." The outrage had turned into acceptance without her noticing.

Ellen lay still. "I'm not making any moves that might not be appreciated. Let's talk about this."

"I never thought those calcium deposits would be anything but benign. Cancer doesn't run in my family. After the surgical procedure, I even forgot to call for the results."

It had been Mary who insisted she phone the oncologist. "I've got to know for peace of mind," Mary said, picking up the receiver and thrusting it at her.

When the surgeon told her the pathologist had found cancer cells in the calcium deposits and that he was recommending a mastectomy, she'd been stunned.

She was quiet long enough for Ellen to glance at her and murmur, "Go on."

The surgery had been scheduled in two weeks.

"I wanted rid of it. As it turned out I could have kept the breast, because it hadn't spread past those tiny deposits. But I don't have to take tamoxifen, nor do I have to undergo radiation or chemo. It's gone, although I guess it could recur. It's unlikely, though."

The open windows were black against the one light on the bedside table. Ellen asked, "How did you feel?"

"Angry, betrayed, humiliated, embarrassed."

"I can understand feeling angry and betrayed, but not the other two."

"My body let me down. I never said it made sense. I didn't want to talk about it."

"Not even to me." Ellen's dark eyes were accusing.

"That would have pinned you in a corner. I let you go instead."

Ellen propped herself on an elbow, facing Josey with her anger. "I suppose you thought you were being noble. Actually, it was rather cruel. No explanation, other than your niece was coming. I had no idea what had happened."

"Hey, give me a little slack here. I wouldn't have believed you if you'd said it made no difference."

"And you believe me now?"

"It's different now. I'm going to have reconstruction soon. I can hide behind these gigantic T-shirts till then. I still don't want to share this with anyone else. You know, Mary knows, my sister knows, my doctors know. Let's keep it that way."

"So, do you want to make love or not?" Ellen asked.

Josey leaned forward and lightly kissed Ellen's mouth. "Let's go slow." This was a crossroads of sorts. She snuggled into Ellen's softness.

"I missed this," Ellen murmured, moving nearer, kissing Josey's face and neck. "You taste wonderful."

"Like leftover wine."

"Fresh, like the outdoors."

"You smell like a muffin. Did you eat at the coffee shop?"

"Yes. Shelley was upset, but we'll talk of that later."

Josey stiffened as Ellen's hand moved under her T-shirt. "I'm not taking my shirt off. Don't go feeling around in there."

"I won't. I'm terrified to look at you for fear you'll be enraged."

Josey whispered as she began a caress, "You are so womanly."

"Another adjective for fat."

"If it's fat, it's the good kind. What's that called? Unsaturated?" She smiled, her lips against Ellen's.

Ellen laughed, a warm explosion in Josey's mouth. "And you have muscles that run the length of your body. How do you stay that way?"

It was Ellen's desire that stirred Josey to passion, that and the months of doing without. She had almost forgotten the pleasure that came with touch. She dripped a few tears on Ellen's breasts, nearly throwing cold water on everything.

Ellen tried to pull Josey's head up. "I'm sorry."

"Why? For having two breasts? Don't take them away." Although she wouldn't allow Ellen to nuzzle hers, she buried her face between Ellen's and breathed deeply.

Ellen ran fingers through her hair and murmured comfort. "It's okay, sweetheart. You have a right to cry."

Josey lifted her head and sniffed. "I'm slobbering all over you."

"I love it. Slobber all you want."

Afterwards Ellen said, "Come on up here and rest a while. I thought we were supposed to go slow."

"Maybe next time," Josey said, suddenly sleepy again. Her eyes closed even as she fought to stay awake.

When she awakened, Ellen lay breathing softly, pinned under one of Josey's arms and legs. She carefully removed herself, unsticking the skin that seemed loath to let go, and Ellen rolled on her side. Snuggling from behind, Josey threw an arm around Ellen and cupped a breast. Sighing with pleasure, she again drifted into sleep.

She awoke to see the shadow of the oak on the wall and ceiling, its leaves shimmering in the warm wind. Except for a cardinal singing, there was no sound.

Ellen opened her eyes and reached for her.

The dog put his paws on the bed. "Buddy has to go out."

XVI
Annie

John dropped her off around one in the morning. Ellen's car was parked next to Josey's. "Looks like you have company."

"I'm sorry I wasn't better company myself."

"Hey, it was a great evening." He had been stoned early on, but a swim and a walk had made him sober enough to drive home. "Want me to walk you to the door?"

"Nope." She was feeling tearful. Molly had turned her back to them both at the Fox.

A light left on over the sink lit her way through the kitchen and up the stairs. She heard a quiet "woof" from behind Josey's closed door. Ellen must be in there with Josey. She hadn't known they were a couple, had thought they were just friends. It made her feel twice as lonely.

She dreamed she heard people talking and walking in the hallway while she was locked in her bedroom, isolated from everyone. Then they were gone and her dreams moved on in silence.

Waking with a start when Molly pulled the sheet off her, she recalled the people outside her door and realized they must have been Josey and Ellen in the early morning.

"What do you want?" she asked Molly.

Molly slid into bed, so that they lay side by side, their arms and thighs touching. "What did you do nights? You and John?"

"Slept. What do you think? And what does it matter anyway? You're always telling me that you and I mean nothing."

"I'm going to L.U. in Appleton in the fall. You'll be at Madison," Molly said, her warm breath on Annie's cheek.

Annie kept her gaze on the ceiling. "Maybe not."

"What are you going to do if you don't go back to the university?"

"I don't know if I'll be able to return or if I want to."

"You just gonna stay here?"

Annie shrugged, feeling she had nowhere to go. "I'll get a job."

"You can visit me in Appleton."

Annie smiled a little. "On my scooter?"

"Look at me." Molly turned Annie's head.

Annie thought of nothing except the mouth under hers, the body pressed against her own. She thrust her hand in Molly's shorts and felt Molly's fingers in her panties. Everything focused on sensations that quickly spilled over into climax.

"You're gay, like me," Annie said afterwards, touching Molly's bare arm as if to claim her.

Molly jerked away. "I did it with Cass while you were gone."

The words felt like stabs, taking her breath away with the pain. "Okay, then what is this between us?"

"Friendship?" Molly said.

Annie laughed harshly to cover the hurt. "Extreme friendship, intense friendship, friendship gone overboard?"

"What are you doing today?" Molly asked.

"I don't know," she said.

125

"I'm going to Cass's cottage. He's got one of those Mastercraft boats with a six cylinder engine. Gets you right out of the water on skis like you weigh nothing. Want to try it?"

"Water skiing? No." It'd kill her ankle. The high brought on by their lovemaking had vanished. She felt flat.

"You could ride in the boat. Be the spotter," Molly said.

"No thanks." Cass had done it with Molly. How could she act as if nothing had happened.

Molly shrugged. "Rog's going to be there. He asked me to pick you up." She leaned toward Annie and whispered, "I'll be here at noon on Monday."

"Whatever," Annie muttered.

"Come on now. Get up. They'll be waiting for us." Molly got to her feet and looked down at Annie. "Let's put on our swimsuits."

"Why would you want me there? You'll have Cass," Annie said sulkily.

"I don't want to be the only female."

"Bullshit," she said as Molly dragged her out of bed. But the alternative to going was staying here, alone, knowing that Molly was with Cass, wondering what was going on between them. "You have to promise to bring me home."

"Cross my heart." Molly traced a little X over her left breast.

They turned into a blacktop drive with a large log house at the end. Getting out of the truck, Annie and Molly took the wood steps down to the lake. Roger and Cass sat in the speedboat, rocking on waves from passing craft. Turning, she looked up at what Cass called a cottage. Two stories of glass beat back the sunlight, a deck spanned the width and one side of the house on the middle floor, glass doors opened to a walkout basement under the deck.

"Roy Schroeder built this palace," Molly said, following her gaze.

"Come on, get in," Cass called from the boat.

Annie sat on a bench seat in the rear of the boat with Rog. Molly took the swivel seat next to Cass. When Cass hit the throttle, the

126

boat surged from the pier, pinning Annie to the cushion. Hot, wet wind washed over her as they rocketed around the lake, passing every other craft. When they drew close to the dock, Cass put the engine into neutral and the boat lost all momentum.

"Molly, you're first."

When Molly rose out of the water on one ski, Annie felt her throat tighten. She would never achieve such grace on water and was awed by it. Then Rog did the same, and Cass used no skis, went instead barefoot, his body lost in a spray of water.

At five-thirty, when lake rules called for all boats to slow down to a crawl, Cass docked the boat and they swam. The water cooled Annie's sunburned skin as she floated in an innertube. The red orb of sun slid closer to the tree-tops.

"Anyone want a beer?" Cass asked, leaping high in the water to throw a tennis ball to Rog.

"Are you the only one staying here?" Annie asked.

"Yep. I'm spending the summer."

"Doing what?" she persisted.

"Shearing Christmas trees. Didn't Molly tell you?"

She lay her head on the back of the tube and closed her eyes. Black dots broke loose behind her lids. Climbing out onto the pier, she spread her towel and lay face down on it.

When Molly woke her, the sun was dipping out of sight. Rog and Cass sat in the boat, drinking beer.

"Want to go home?" Molly asked.

"Yes." Her head spun when she got to her feet to gather her things. She said her thanks and climbed the stairs to Molly's truck. She'd never seen the inside of the house.

"You don't look so hot," Molly said.

"Too much sun, I think."

When Molly dropped her off, only the Escort was in the drive-way. "Want to stay awhile? We could take a walk."

"It's late. I told Dad I'd be home for supper."

"You're a wonderful skier."

"I've had lots of practice. Your turn next."

Yeah, right, she thought. "See you."

"Monday," Molly promised.

Grasshoppers leaped out of the tall grass as Annie made her way to the house. She skirted clumps of daylilies. Buddy shot toward her. As she bent to pat him, the headache lurking in the back of her skull leaped to the fore. She felt like a piece of burnt toast and was in desperate need of a drink of water.

Smiling at Josey drew her skin tight and opened cracks in her lips.

"God, where were you? You look like an over-ripe tomato," Josey said.

"On a boat." She poured herself a glass of water and drained it in a few gulps.

"Hungry? I'm making Chinese chicken salad."

"Sure." She swallowed a couple of ibuprofen. "You alone?"

"I don't see anybody else's car," Josey said.

"Ellen was here when I came home last night."

"You were very late. No wonder you don't look well. Are you staying home tonight?"

"I think so." Annie washed her hands and set the table for two. "Is there time for a shower?"

"Lots of time," Josey said.

When she looked out the bathroom window, she saw her aunt in the garden, picking lettuce. Josey was a mystery to Annie: gruffly terse at times, sarcastically witty at others, rarely tender. Annie wondered what a woman like Ellen would glean from a relationship with her aunt.

She stood watching till Josey and Buddy headed toward the house. Her aunt's voice carried to her on the wind, but not clear enough to understand. She was baby-talking to the dog, who jumped like a pogo stick in response. This was the aunt she rarely saw.

Supper killed her headache and gave her a little energy. "I think I'll go for a scooter ride when the dishes are done, if that's okay."

"Hey, it's your scooter for the duration. It's a lovely night."

She wandered up and down the blacktop roads, crossing the same trout stream as it meandered, spotting lakes through the side yards of cottages, passing woods and fields where deer grazed. The sun slid out of sight and the moon rose. She followed it home.

The next morning Josey helped her set up the ladder before leaving. Flexing her ankle, Annie felt only a small ache.

She was used to the natural sounds now. The frogs croaking from the pond at night, the birds marking their territories by song during the day, and now the high-pitched buzzing of insects. She no longer missed the sounds of traffic and people.

Binding her ankle with the Ace bandage, she climbed the ladder stiffly, paint in one hand, brush in the other. It was monotonous work. Every few feet she had to move the ladder.

She'd gone about twenty-some feet when Molly drove in and walked across the thin grass to stand next to the ladder. "I can't stay long," she called.

Annie made her way down the narrow steps. Her ankle had no give and ached fiercely. She tapped the cover onto the can of paint and put the brush in a plastic bag.

"I thought you weren't coming till Monday," she said as they washed their hands in the upstairs bathroom.

Molly tweaked paint from Annie's hair. "Want me to leave? Whose car was that parked in your drive yesterday?"

"Ellen, the librarian." She followed Molly to the bedroom and closed the door behind them.

"Oh, yeah," Molly said knowingly. "She and your aunt had a thing going before you came."

"Do you know what cooled them off?" Annie pulled her T-shirt off and dropped it on the floor. She wore nothing under it.

"Not a clue." Molly stood naked.

Annie took a deep pleasurable breath. "You're beautiful. Yesterday's burn is already turning brown." She knew her burn would peel off and leave a few more freckles on her shoulders.

Molly put warm hands over Annie's breasts. "Come on. Lie down." They were getting better at knowing where and how to touch. It wasn't over almost before it began anymore. They managed to hang on for a good ten minutes. Annie knew because she timed their love-making. Satisfied, she rolled away and stared at a cobweb hanging from the overhead light, lazily moving in the open window's breeze.

Molly lifted herself onto an elbow, her thick hair covering the hand holding her head. "Have you thought about what you're going to do about school? We could share an apartment or a dorm room at Appleton."

"I can't afford a private college," she snorted. "I'll be here, earning money for next year."

"You could move to Appleton and get a job."

Molly hadn't jumped out of bed after the act and fled as she usually did. Annie caressed her cheek with the back of her hand.

Molly smiled and smacked a kiss on her lips. "Got to go."

The afternoon went by slowly. Snatches of clouds blew overhead. From the direction of the pond she heard what Josey said were sand-hill cranes. Blue jays screeched in the pines. They were out-voiced by a flock of crows cawing endlessly. Josey had told her when crows carried on like that they were usually badgering an owl or a hawk.

She quit painting around four when her ankle throbbed too much to ignore and black spots burst behind her lids. Carefully, she climbed off the ladder as John drove in.

"How you doing?" he asked, his hair aflame in the afternoon sun.

"I've been better. How was the showing? Was Monty a star?" She hammered the lid on the paint can and took the brush inside to wash.

"We did well. So did Candy. What did you do yesterday?"

"I spotted for Cass and Rog and Molly. I don't know how to water-ski." She squeezed moisture out of the brush and placed it on the counter. "Want a Pepsi?"

"Yeah. Thanks." He sat at the table, a sunburst of red hair and skin. "How's the ankle?"

She pulled out a chair across from him and placed her lame ankle on another. "It aches like crazy right now."

"I've got the week free. Want some help?"

That would mean no Molly at noon. She weighed the pros and cons. "Are you sure?"

He drank the Pepsi in a few gulps and smiled at her. "Actually, I like painting. I'll bring another ladder."

"Thanks. You are a love."

"That's my name." He bent over and kissed her cheek.

The following day, she and John were on ladders, painting in companionable silence, when Molly drove in. Annie's ears pricked at the sound, her heart banged with worry, her skin and eyes burned from the sun.

Molly looked up at Annie. "Got some help, huh?"

"Hey, Molly. What are you doing here?" John asked. "Did you bring lunch?"

"I'll fix lunch," Annie said, climbing down, hoping for a moment of privacy with Molly.

In the kitchen, Molly said, "Did you ask him for help?"

"He offered. It's just this one week." She heard the plea in her voice. "I'll never get done otherwise."

"Why do you want to finish? Then what will you do?" Molly asked.

She realized then that as soon as the house was painted and she went elsewhere to work, their noontime trysts would end. "You'll be gone before I'm finished here."

The afternoon flew by. Annie's spirits picked up as they finished the south side of the house. John moved the ladders around to the western exposure. Around four they quit. He had to feed the horses and clean stalls. She was lightheaded, her ankle aching.

Josey found her on the porch, a beer trickling like a cool sedative down her throat and through her veins.

"You made great progress," her aunt said.

"John helped," she told Josey.

XVII
Josey

She painted Candy and Snipper's portrait during gallery hours. The easel faced the windows overlooking the mill pond. Customers made their way around the room and stopped to watch her and ask questions.

Candy and her mother came in and studied the portrait Monday morning.

"Cool," Candy said. "I'm immortalized, and look at Snippers. She's noble."

"It is wonderful," Reenie agreed. "How much longer, do you think?"

"It should be done by the end of the week. I'll call you."

"We'll pick it up. You don't have to bring it out," Reenie said.

"How'd you do at the show this weekend?" Josey asked.

"Candy and Snippers won the amateur all-around," Reenie said proudly. "We thought maybe we'd let Monty make Snippers a mama early next spring." Reenie smiled at her daughter.

"I'd like to see the baby," Josey said. She pictured a grown-up-looking foal, a cross between Monty and Snippers.

"You can paint him or her," Reenie promised.

When Reenie and Candy left, Josey rose and stretched. It was close to noon, almost time for Ellen to arrive with lunch and Mary to emerge from the back room where she was throwing some serious pottery.

She looked at the pond, shimmering in the sun, the edges green with algae. A mama mallard and six ducklings paddled by. Three red-eared turtles sunned on a downed stub of a tree.

The door creaked open for Ellen. "Lunch lady," she announced, putting the stuff on the counter. Her smile glimmered in the depths of her eyes.

A grin tugged at the corners of Josey's mouth. "Come on out, Mary," she called, pulling up a stool across from Ellen.

"The buyers would like to take their purchases home from the library. So how about replacing some of the stuff," Ellen said when Mary emerged from the studio. "The exhibit goes through the second week in July."

Clay spotted Mary's face, neck, and shirt. "That's great. How about exhibiting the *Woman in Blue*, Jose?"

"It's not the right place," Josey said. "Think of all those little kids."

"There will never be a right place," Mary pointed out, smearing cream cheese on a bagel.

"Maybe one of the galleries in Appleton or Oshkosh would agree to an art show featuring the two of you. You should look into it."

Josey and Mary exchanged glances. Marketing was not their thing.

"Or I could look into it." Bright-eyed with enthusiasm, Ellen glanced from one to the other.

Josey held back as she always did when her work was put to public scrutiny, worried that it wouldn't measure up.

"Wouldn't that be great, Josey?" Mary enthused. "It's worth a try."

"Somebody'll be interested. I'd bet on it." Ellen tore her bagel in half and eyed Josey. "Consider exhibiting the *Woman in Blue*. Nobody will think it's you."

Mary cleared off the counter before returning to the back room. "I'm going to fire this plate."

Josey and Ellen were left staring at each other across the counter. "I brought you a book." Ellen smiled hesitantly.

"Another mystery." She hefted the book. "Got any new ones by Sue Grafton?"

"Wish I did, but no. Any chance on your coming over tonight?"

She pictured Annie home alone, the garden being neglected, Buddy waiting for her. She fudged. "Maybe after dinner, I could drive in for a while."

"Why don't you stay the night?"

She scanned Ellen's eyes, not at all sure this was what she wanted. Reluctant to commit herself, she felt pressed to give it a try.

"Bring Buddy with you. We can go for a walk."

That clinched it for her. The dog would be a buffer of sorts. She hadn't realized till then that she was a little afraid of Ellen's persistent pursuit of her. She feared losing herself in a joining that might compromise her independence.

After Ellen left, Josey resumed her painting. She was putting color to the horse's head when it came time to close up shop.

Mary emerged from the studio, wiping her hands on a gray towel. "Want to go out for dinner?"

Josey said, "I'm going to Ellen's after dinner tonight."

"Call her and ask her to join us. You can go over there afterwards. Let's call Shelley, too." Mary nudged her with an elbow. "Are you finally getting a social life?"

She nudged back. "Are you?" Mary made a better buffer than Buddy. "You call them. I better call home first."

The roads to the Crystal Supper Club on Crystal Lake just outside of the town with the same name wound past small lakes. Deer grazed in the meadows at the edges of oak and pine woods. Sandhill cranes stalked through the grasses in family groups of three or four. Mary slowed for a flock of wild turkeys, hens with chicks, crossing the road. Heads bobbing, they hurried with anxious gobbles into the woods on the other side.

Josey and Ellen sat in the back of Mary's Taurus, blown by warm air from the open windows.

Shelley rode in the passenger seat next to Mary. "What a great idea. My youngest son asked, 'What are we supposed to eat, Ma.' And I said, 'Whatever you want to fix.'"

"Way to go. Teach those boys to be independent. Their wives will appreciate them." Mary slammed on the brakes as a doe and two fawns leaped onto the road. "Damn deer. Why can't they look both ways?"

Ellen said, "You should see the carcasses on the way to La Crosse. Every half mile or so there's roadkill."

Shelley went on, "There are no wives looming in the near future, that I met anyway. Do you have any idea what it's like to have six guys in the house and not one cooks, picks up after himself, or puts the toilet lid down? Despite all my nagging. But then I never have to mow the lawn, shovel snow, take out the garbage, clean gutters, or paint." She laughed loudly. "Still, they're a lot of work."

"Damn men," Mary shouted over the wind flowing through the Taurus.

They parked in the lot near the huge bull statue, balls and all, out by the road. Stepping into the smoky, boozy atmosphere, Mary left their names with the hostess. They headed for the bar.

Finding a place near the bank of windows facing the lake was impossible, so they settled for one of the rear tables around the dance floor. They paused to talk to the police chief, Bernie Protheroe, and his wife, Cindy.

"Now we'll have to behave," Shelley said.

"Is this girls' night out?" Bernie asked.

"You should join us, Cindy," Mary suggested.

"I wouldn't mind," Cindy said.

"Thanks a lot," Bernie put in. "You girls behave yourselves."

"I know I'm getting old when I appreciate being referred to as a girl," Ellen observed.

"Me too." What Josey wanted was a cigarette. She'd kept her promise to herself not to buy any and only occasionally bummed one off someone. Usually Roy when she ran into him, but she hadn't seen him for a long time.

When Shelley pulled a pack out of her purse and offered it around, Josey brightened and took one. "I thought you gave up smoking."

"I did. I only smoke on special occasions, like this," Shelley explained.

"Don't blow it my way," Mary said. "I don't want any secondhand smoke."

Ellen shook her head at Shelley's offer. "Not my thing."

They ordered a round of drinks and ate the stale popcorn in the basket on the table while they looked around the room.

"Don't see anyone I know except Bernie and Cindy," Mary commented.

Half an hour later, they carried their drinks to their table in the dining room overlooking the lake. Outside, kids swam and played in the sand. Speedboats motored by, pulling skiers.

"Makes me wish I were out there," Ellen said, sipping a gin and tonic.

"It seems like I never get out on the lake anymore," Mary mused. Her home fronted Pine Lake.

"Come winter I'd like to go somewhere warm, like Mexico," Josey said. She glanced at Ellen. There had been no one to go anywhere with for years. She and Mary couldn't be gone at the same time, not even for a few days.

Ellen smiled at her. "That'd be nice."

They watched the lake take on the colors of the sunset as they ate. Boats paraded slowly offshore. Kids still played on the beach and in the water, their parents either with them or watching from benches.

"They do that at Pine Lake, too. Every night if it's not cold or rainy, people drive their boats around the shoreline. I guess it's happy hour on water."

They were downing the last of the wine now and ordered decaffeinated coffee. Josey felt pleasantly drowsy.

"Maybe we should get a room," Mary said.

"I doubt they'll have a vacancy," Josey remarked, "not this time of year."

"We can ask, rather than drive back to Clover after all that liquor and wine."

"Let's," Shelley said. "It'll be fun."

Ellen shrugged an okay.

When they walked out into the dark night, Josey and Ellen paused to look at the stars and breathe fresh air. The smell of the lake drifted shoreward on a soft breeze. Without a word, the two of them headed toward an empty bench nearby.

"I wish all nights were like this," Ellen said.

"It makes winter seem far away."

"It is," Ellen said, her face pale in the dim light. "Would you really like to go to Mexico, say next February or March?"

"Of course, but I can't afford to. It's a dream."

"Not an impossible one, though."

"I guess not." She'd always loved the ocean.

"Guess what?" Mary joined them with Shelley. "They have a room with two double beds."

"You're the driver," Josey said. "If it's all right with everyone else, it's okay with me."

"I'll go get another bottle of wine," Shelley offered, then disappeared into the bar.

"It's room thirty. Come when you're ready. I'll register," Mary said.

When Josey and Ellen joined the other two, they found Shelley and Mary watching a not very good movie on HBO. Shelley and Mary sat on one bed, Ellen and Josey took the other. The others dressed down to underpants and shirts; Josey wasn't about to remove the shirt whose pocket she'd stuffed with tissues.

Before the movie ended, Josey slid under the sheet and fell into a light sleep. She heard the murmur of voices. At three in the morning, her eyes opened.

No one had drawn the drapes. The waning moon hung low over the lake. Ellen breathed quietly at her side. Soft snoring came from the other bed.

She rose quietly and went to the bathroom. Finding her own small pile of clothes, she put them on. Grabbing the key from the dresser, she let herself out of the room.

The night was warm, and she waded in the lake now empty of swimmers and watercraft. Sitting on a bench near the water, she watched the moon drop behind the treeline across the lake. The sky began to lighten and a few birds gave tentative chirps.

Unlocking the door to the room, she crept inside and climbed back into bed. Slightly chilled, she moved close to Ellen.

XVIII
Annie

By the end of the week, John and Annie had finished putting the primer on the house except for the highest story. That Josey forbade. She said she'd hire someone to do it.

The place now needed a coat of exterior latex on top of the primer. Annie felt as if she'd been doing this forever, that it was never going to end.

"I'll be back to help," John promised Friday morning. He had a horse show over the weekend to get ready for.

"God, I hope so." She smiled at his red face and ears, liking him. "Break a leg tomorrow. Beat those trainers."

"I'll try. Want me to pick you up tonight?"

"You bet." She touched his arm, pink and freckled and muscular. "You're the best."

"Yeah, sure." But he looked pleased.

After he left, she called the hardware store. Molly's dad answered. Molly was out on deliveries. She was so horny it was all she could do to keep her hands to herself, but she didn't want to take the edge off. She had one gallon of exterior white and decided to start again. Putting the ballcap on backwards to keep the sun off her neck, she began on the south side. Crows cawed from the woods, blue jays screeched. From a distance she heard machinery and wondered if it was Roy and his crew working on his Barkins Woods home.

Tires crunching down the driveway raised goosebumps on her back and arms and neck. She turned to look.

Molly sauntered across the yard, her hands in her back pockets and a sexy smile on her face. "You're alone."

"Yep. It's been a long week."

Still partially dressed, they hurried through sex. After, they lay in the hot room, panting, gathering strength. She heard the footsteps on the stairs and in the second-floor hallway, she realized later, but failed to register the warning.

When her aunt's surprised, "Oh," came from the doorway, Annie felt as if she'd been doused in water, so cold it burned. She and Molly sprang apart as the door closed on them.

Annie fell back on the bed with a moan. "Oh my God, I think I'll die."

Molly turned her head, her brown hair splayed across the quilt. "You won't be that lucky. You don't think she'd tell my dad, do you?"

"No, but I have to look her in the face." She writhed a little at the thought. "How am I going to do that?"

"I think I better sneak out of here," Molly whispered, leaning over to plant a kiss on Annie before jumping to her feet.

"Sure, abandon me." Annie got up to dress. "I need some exterior white. I'm almost out."

"You better come in and get it yourself."

"John's picking me up tonight. You going to be at the Fox?" Annie hoped her aunt would go back to the Mill if they dallied enough.

"I'll be there." Molly smacked her lightly on the ass. "Walk me out of here. I'm not going alone."

"Fuck," Annie said, "just when I was really getting into it."

"Me, too."

But Josey's door was shut when they went into the hallway. They tiptoed downstairs.

Annie's scalp prickled as she walked across the yard to Molly's truck, sure that Josey was watching from her bedroom window. "Maybe I'll get the scooter out and ride into town for the paint." That would be better than facing Josey.

Molly laughed. "See you tonight, girlfriend. I've got deliveries to do." She backed around and drove off.

Sitting on the Honda Spree, Annie glanced at the house before starting the scooter. As she clamped the ballcap tightly on her head, Josey walked into the yard and cupped her hands around her mouth.

"Helmet," her aunt yelled.

She went back into the garage. The helmet hung on a wheelbarrow handle. Loud cheeps came from its depths. She peeked inside at three tiny open beaks. She left them there and climbed, helmetless, on the scooter and turned the key.

Josey had gone back in the house. Swinging the bike in a wide circle, she drove out of the yard. She loved riding the scooter on hot days, the hot wind in her face, the pungent odor of things growing. She wondered if she'd remember this summer as an aroma.

It took a good half hour to get to Clover on the scooter, even though it was only ten miles away. She parked in front of the hardware store as Josey pulled in behind her.

"Where's the helmet?" her aunt asked, getting out of the Escort.

Annie felt her face redden. "There are baby birds in it."

"Then you'll have to wait till they've flown to ride the Spree." The corners of Josey's mouth twitched.

"How am I gonna get home?"

"Go straight there and stay put."

At least there was no time to talk, Annie thought. She entered the coolness of the hardware store. Molly's dad was stacking shelves. She was glad that it hadn't been he who'd caught her and his daughter in the act. Her ears burned again at what her aunt must have seen.

She put the paint in the plastic carton fastened behind the scooter's seat with tarp hooks. She took another route home and was passing Barkins Woods when Roy waved her down.

"When did you get new wheels, Annie?" he asked when she pulled into the rutted driveway.

"I don't have the Jeep anymore. This is Josey's scooter."

"It looks like fun." She liked Roy despite the gossip about him, or maybe because of it. He fished an envelope out of his shirt pocket and handed it to her. "Give this to your aunt, will you? If she wants to talk about it, she can call me."

There was no sign of Roy's crew. "Is the house done?" It rose out of a small hill, big and raw.

"Done enough for me to move in," he said. "How's the painting job?"

"John Lovelace helped me finish the priming. Now I have to start all over with regular paint. It never ends."

"John's okay." He smiled, showing white teeth and dimples. "Thanks for stopping."

"Josey caught me in town without a helmet. I was supposed to go straight home."

"You should wear a helmet. Don't want to bang up that pretty head."

She felt a blush coming on. "Baby birds are nesting in it."

"Guess you temporarily lost your wheels."

She was painting when her aunt drove in and walked to the ladder. Looking down, Annie met Josey's eyes briefly before turning away.

"I'm sorry you saw us like that," she blurted, her face burning.

When Josey said nothing for a moment, Annie glanced at her worriedly. She caught a smile on her aunt's upturned face.

"It's okay, kiddo," Josey said and then laughed. "You can come down now."

After supper, Josey sat on the porch with Annie.

"Does John know?" Josey asked.

"No, but he's never even tried to kiss me."

Josey asked, "How serious is this thing with Molly?"

"I don't know," Annie said, avoiding her aunt's eyes.

"Exactly."

Annie made brief eye contact before dropping her gaze. "What does that mean?"

"She probably doesn't know either. You're both young." Josey was quiet for a moment. "It's so very sweet while it lasts, but when it's over, it hurts like hell."

"Thanks for the warning," Annie said.

"Any time you want to talk, I'm ready to listen." She pulled the envelope Roy had given Annie out of her pocket. "Did Roy bring this over?"

"He flagged me down at his new house and gave it to me. He said if you wanted to talk about it to give him a call."

"I'll do that," she said.

John's Bronco rolled to a stop in front of the garage. Annie threw a shy glance at her aunt. "Thanks."

Josey squeezed her hand, then quickly let go. "See you tomorrow."

"Are you going to be here tonight?"

"I think I'll just pop over to Barkins Woods and see if I can catch Roy."

John had walked to within talking distance of the porch. "Hi, Josey," he called.

"Nice job on the house. Thanks, John."

"It's just the beginning. We do good work, don't we, Annie?" He waved as Annie joined him.

As they crossed the yard to his vehicle, Annie was thinking she should feel about John the way she felt about Molly. She longed to talk to Josey, to have Josey to tell her she was normal. Her aunt was a loner, an artist, and a lesbian. Anything Josey had to tell her would only confirm Annie's own opinion of herself.

"You're quiet," John said when they swung out of the driveway onto the road. "Everything okay?"

"Yeah, sure." Everything except the fact that she was queer and oversexed. "Did you have a girlfriend at the university?"

His ears turned pinker. "Yeah." He smiled and shrugged. "We had a really cool thing going. When I didn't hear from her, I was sure it was over, but then I got a letter this week. I was going to tell you."

"That's great, John. Tell me about her."

He pulled a photo from his shirt pocket and handed it to Annie. She studied it carefully. A girl with straight brown hair and serious eyes behind glasses. She looked like a brain. "Is she in pre-vet, too?" She handed back the picture and watched him tuck it away.

"Yep. We've talked about going into practice together."

"That's wonderful, John." It should have taken a load of worry off her. Instead, she felt slightly left out. What was the matter with her that he preferred this homely girl? Wasn't she better looking? Didn't she and John have a lot of fun together?

It made her wonder what attracted two people to each other. In her case, there were not a lot of choices. How many lesbians were there in Clover? Not enough to pass up someone like Molly.

"I hope we can still be friends," John said.

Annie replied seriously. "I'll always think of you as my friend."

They parked under lights flickering on and made their way to the door of the bar. The sun streaked the sky with pinks and reds and purples. Annie thought it a shame to leave the clean smell of pines and lake and go into the beery, smoky interior. But Molly was inside.

Fall

XIX
Josey

She sat in a recliner in Recovery, waiting for the doctor and wondering where Mary was. Mary had brought her in for reconstructive surgery that morning. When the plastic surgeon slid into a chair, she smiled, glad the surgery was over, pleased to be on her way to a balanced body.

"How are you feeling?" he asked.

"A little groggy, but all right," she said.

He patted her on the knee, his face kind. "We didn't put the skin stretcher in. The scar tissue looked suspect, so I removed some for biopsy. I thought that was better than going ahead without knowing. We should have the results by Friday."

Stunned, she stared into his pale blue eyes. Fear spread through her. "What?" She'd been told the cancer hadn't spread beyond the few ducts, that the odds of recurrence, although always possible, were extremely small. She'd thought she was safe. Tears choked her throat and blurred her vision.

Mary appeared in the curtained cubicle.

"Mary Durban. Dr. Lieberman." She blinked her eyes clear.

Mary stepped forward to shake hands.

"Go ahead. Tell her. I probably won't remember everything." She knew from last time that the anesthetic lingered.

He did. Then said, "A week from today, we'll take off the bandages and remove the drainage tube." Patting Josey on the knee again, he gave her another kindly smile. "If someone doesn't call you by Friday, phone the office."

Mary looked as stunned as Josey felt. She put a hand on Josey's shoulder and squeezed. When the doctor left, she said, "You'll be all right, sweetie," as if saying it could make it true.

Josey knew she'd never really feel safe again. A nurse wheeled her to the entrance doors of the Outpatient Center. Mary opened the door for her, and she walked from the wheelchair to the passenger side of the vehicle.

Mary glanced at her several times before saying fiercely, "Well, that sucks."

As they crossed Little Lake Butte des Morts, an eagle flared against the sky, but Josey was too disheartened to point it out.

Mary took her hand. "It'll be all right. Didn't the oncologist tell you that it hadn't spread, that the chances of recurrence were almost zip?"

"Yes." In the beginning, she'd been so sure there was nothing to worry about. She wouldn't forget to call about the biopsy results this time. Three days. She opened the window farther. The sun shone down. The warm air smelled of fall. She pictured herself in a chemotherapy room, hooked up to one of those poison-dispensing machines. Would she rather die?

Mary said, "Roy's right down the road from you. Maybe you should let him in on this now that Annie's gone. He's quite fond of you."

Annie had followed Molly into Appleton in early September. She lived off campus and worked as a waitress in one of the downtown restaurants. "I don't need a keeper yet."

"I know, but Roy's five minutes away."

"Did I tell you he wouldn't accept my money for putting a new foundation under the garage?"

"Didn't you pay for the cement?"

"Yes, but for nothing else."

"You didn't ask him to do it, did you?"

"No, and that's another thing. He was making my decisions for me."

"Josey, the garage was about to fall over. Don't be so proud. It's an everyday job for him."

"Too many people know now."

"Who? Me, your sister, Ellen. That's too many people? It's not like you committed some stupid *faux pas*, like picking your nose in public. Millions of women get breast cancer."

"You'd keep it quiet, too, if it were you. You wouldn't let the whole town in on it."

"Okay, calm down. Want a cup of coffee?" They were nearing Winchester.

"French vanilla cappuccino, a big one."

"Be right out." Mary parked in front of the Kwik Trip station and jumped out of the car.

Josey fell asleep before she finished drinking the cappuccino. She awakened when the truck turned into her driveway. The freshly painted house loomed a stark white, rising out of the thin, tall grass. It hurt the eyes.

"Why won't you come home with me?" Mary asked.

"I'll be all right."

"Then I'll stay the night here." Mary helped her out of the Taurus.

She had no more pain than she'd had after the mastectomy,

maybe less. She made her way across the yard as Buddy danced around her in maniacal circles.

"Damn dog'll trip you up. He's always so flipping glad to see everybody." Mary laughed and slid a hand under Josey's elbow.

The phone was ringing in the kitchen. Mary grabbed it and listened a moment, letting Josey shuffle over to a chair on her own. "We just got back. Come on over."

"Who?" Josey asked as Mary hung up.

"Ellen. You want something to eat?" she asked. "Toast?"

She hadn't finished the muffin they'd given her at the hospital. "If you wouldn't mind. And orange juice. On the porch."

No chemo, please, she prayed to the God of her childhood, the one who surfaced during crises. Her abandoned Protestant upbringing surprised her in times of distress. It lurked under the surface of her professed agnosticism, as if it had never been rejected.

She lowered herself into the recliner on the porch. The pines smelled strong. Screeching blue jays sailed through branches fluttering in a warm breeze. Cardinals, chickadees, and goldfinches vied for a spot on the feeders.

The sun hung low over the treetops when she awakened. Someone had covered her. Gathering the blanket around her shoulders, she dragged it inside.

Mary and Ellen looked up from the table. Ellen said, "I couldn't stay away."

"Who's minding the store?" she asked.

"To hell with the store. We'll brave this one out together." Mary popped the cork on a bottle of wine. "First, wine for me and Ellen, then dinner for all."

It was Ellen who spent the night with her. "Maybe it would be better if I slept in another room."

Josey patted the empty side of the bed. "Just get your ass in here."

She needed the comfort and wished she'd taken advantage of what

Ellen had to offer months ago, before the mastectomy. All those nights spent crying alone. Not that she was going to cry anymore, at least not until she knew she had something to shed tears over.

She watched Ellen undress, although she herself had changed into her nightclothes in the bathroom.

Ellen slid under the sheet. "Do you want to talk?"

"I don't want chemo. I don't want to take tamoxifen." She desperately wanted what she'd had only a few days ago, freedom from uncertainty.

Ellen put an arm over her. "Is this all right? I'm not hurting you?"

"It doesn't hurt. It feels like a piece of cardboard, just like it did before." But there was the drain and cup, which she'd emptied in the bathroom. She'd have to bathe in the tub until the bandage and drainage were removed, which was a pain in the butt.

Josey, who often found sleep so hard to come by, drifted off with Ellen's arm over her, her warm breath on Josey's cheek. In the early morning as gray light filtered through the windows and cool air threaded its way through the screens, she opened her eyes. Ellen's back was turned and Josey fitted herself as close as she dared. The drainage cup lay between them.

Mary called to say she would spend the night with her, that Ellen had to work late at the library. Josey opened her mouth to say she was all right, that she could sleep alone. She said instead, "Okay."

"It'll be like a slumber party. It's comforting to have someone in bed, don't you think?"

"You didn't sleep with me after the last surgery."

"I should have. I wanted to."

Josey was on the porch with the portable phone she'd bought with some of the portrait money. One horse picture had led to another. She'd put away a sizable chunk.

She smiled at the thought of Mary in her bed. When she first knew Mary, she'd dreamed of such a thing. Now she knew she wouldn't be able to get past the friendship to something more, even if there was a chance. Which there wasn't.

That night she and Mary sat around the kitchen table, chewing on steaks Mary had broiled. "A little tough," Mary admitted. She didn't pretend to be a good cook.

"Good exercise for the jaws," Josey said, hoping that an appetite was a sign of health. "Who came into the shop today?"

"Ellen, Shelley, Roy, the bank president's wife, Reenie."

"What did they want?"

"Ellen had lunch with me. Shelley dropped in to say Tom was coming home nights. Roy got the divorce papers. And Reenie bought a painting of yours and a plate of mine."

"What painting, what plate?"

Mary told her. "I thought you'd be pleased," she said when Josey smiled. "You know all these people would bring over food and offer to help in any way they could, if you'd just let them. Roy wanted to know where you were."

"It was peaceful on the porch, watching the birds and reading." Actually, her concentration was shot. "I want to go back to work tomorrow."

Mary studied her. "Kind of soon, isn't it?"

"I can't sit around." She needed something to distract her.

When they climbed into bed that night, Josey knew she wasn't going to sleep. She had taken only ibuprofen for the pain. The prescribed medication nauseated her.

So, they played cribbage.

"I met someone," Mary confessed with a flicker of dark eyes on Josey. She shuffled and dealt.

"Who?"

"His name's Terry MacMillan. He goes by Mac. He's a little younger than I am."

"How much younger?" Josey asked, picking up her hand.

"Fifteen years."

Josey's mouth dropped open. "Tell me about him."

"He's a DNR warden. He loved your painting of the mergansers on the millpond. I think he's going to buy it."

Josey peppered Mary with questions. "What does he look like? Does he have any kids? Where does he live?"

"Tall, dark, outdoorsy. Never been married. Lives near the DNR station."

"Does Roy know?"

Mary shook her dark hair and frowned. "No. And it's none of his business either. Don't tell him."

They finished the game, Mary crowing a little about her win before putting the board and cards away. "Time to sleep, at least for me."

Outside, a great horned owl hooted and another answered. Josey lay awake a long time before Mary's even breathing lulled her to sleep.

The next morning they drove into Clover, one behind the other. Asters nodded in the ditches. Goldenrod stood tall in the fields. The Mill was cool, peaceful. Pale light flowed through the windows. Flipping on the track lights, Josey headed for the easel. On it was the first sketch of the last painting of the *Woman in the Mirror*. She didn't know how the reconstruction would look. She did understand the woman's vulnerability. It showed in her face, her shoulders. She could be brought down again, betrayed by her body.

XX
Annie

Cut loose from adult supervision, basking in freedom, Annie felt she walked just above the ground. She'd rented a furnished room off campus where Molly spent most of her nights. They slept with arms and legs entwined, awakening in the morning sometimes with dry lips touching.

Josey had served as a reference, had helped her move, had given her the scooter to use.

"Come back whenever you want. Your room will be waiting," Josey said before leaving.

She toed the ground outside the three-story rooming house. "Mom's not happy with me."

"I know," Josey had replied. "Audit some courses. That'll bring her around and do you some good at the same time. Whenever you want to come home, I'll come get you," she'd promised.

The offer cheered Annie immeasurably.

She had enough money saved up to audit a creative writing class. That's where she was headed on this golden September morning. She kicked through the leaves fallen at her feet, washed from the trees during a rainstorm the previous evening.

Sliding into a vacant desk at the back of the classroom, she scribbled on a legal pad while waiting. Dr. Fletcher came in with the stragglers, closing the door behind her. Annie raised her eyes and straightened her back. Fletcher's slightly unruly, light brown hair curled around her ears. Her unflinching steely blue eyes demanded truth in writing, or so Annie thought.

Annie woke up on Tuesdays and Thursdays, the days Fletcher's class met, in a state of joyous angst. Joyous because she was learning about plot and dialogue and characterization. Anxious because Fletcher was a tough teacher, expecting her students to put forth their best efforts. Annie was lucky; she didn't have four or five other classes. Fletcher was beginning to notice her writing, to single her out to read. This excited her. She spent her evenings writing and rewriting while Molly bent over her books, sometimes falling asleep.

"Who wants to read today?" Fletcher's thin eyebrows arched. The assignment had been to write a short short story. She pointed a finger at a young man. "Mr. Boyer."

Annie held back, knowing that the heat generated by the sound of her own voice reading her own words flowed first to her skin. Her eyes glittered, her heart pounded, a vocal tremor sometimes gave away her nervousness.

Boyer stood to read. Annie admired his assuredness, but she never liked his stories. They were always about hunting or fishing. In this one he was sitting in a skiff with his black lab, waiting for a good shot at a duck. The day was cold, a skim of ice on the water near the shore. When a smattering of wood ducks banked to land, Annie cringed awaiting the bullet that would smash through one of the male's gaudy feathers.

When Boyer sat down, Fletcher asked for comments.

Several hands shot up. "Action verbs." "Good characterization." "Vivid setting."

Fletcher nodded her head. "Anyone else?"

Annie raised her hand. "Limited appeal."

Fletcher cocked her head and pursed her lips. "True, but can any story appeal to all?" Instead of waiting for an answer, she called on Annie to read.

As she listened to herself, Annie became engulfed in a red haze. She realized her story about the conflict between a girl and a stepfather also had limited appeal.

When asked for comments, Boyer's hand flew up. "Limited appeal. Nevertheless, pretty riveting."

"True," Fletcher said, and pointed to someone else to read. There were only fifteen in the class, yet there was never enough time for everyone to read.

When Annie stuffed her things into her backpack at the end of the two-hour session, Boyer strolled over to her. He was a big guy— broad shouldered, tall, with narrow eyes and thinning hair that she knew would be gone from the top in a few years.

"Call me Jake or Boyer. Just don't call me mister."

"I'm Annie." She responded to his smile with one of her own.

"You don't hunt or fish, do you?" He looked amused.

"Nope, but that was a stupid thing to say. Everyone's stories are limited to what they know. Yours are so real I flinch for whatever you're hunting."

"Would you submit something to the *Campus Review*?"

"I'm just auditing this class. I'm not a student."

"That doesn't matter," he said. "The story you read would do."

"Let me see what I've got at home." She knew what she had written. Her stories stayed in her head long after they were finished. She wanted to submit something less personal.

As she headed for the door, Jake joined the students gathering around Fletcher. She wanted to be one of them but felt she had nothing important to ask or say. She'd feel like an eavesdropper.

Outside in the yellow haze of September, she plunked down on a bench and opened the novel she'd borrowed from the library. Later she would decide what to submit to the magazine and what controversial character she would create for the next writing assignment.

She heard the approaching steps, softened by grass and leaves, and expected them to pass. She raised her eyes only when the bench moved under someone else's weight. Her heart jumped with alarm when she found herself looking into Fletcher's gaze.

"Why aren't you a student, Ms. Spitz?"

Annie shrugged. "No money."

"What about a scholarship? Have you applied?"

"I had a scholarship to Madison. I lost it. Anyway, all I want to do is read books and write."

Fletcher stared across the green and sighed. "How did you lose the scholarship?"

"I was suspended after being arrested at a party. One of the students overdosed on alcohol and died. I was underage." Her voice faded away. She wouldn't meet Fletcher's eyes.

"I heard about that party. You were unfortunate to be one of the fallouts."

"I'm twenty-one now," she said, wondering if that would have made a difference. She pictured the guy in a seizure, vomit dribbling out of the corner of his mouth. "Call me Annie."

"Would you like to be in my creative writing seminar next semester, Annie? I can manage that." When the penetrating eyes lit on her, Annie's gaze slid away. "I invite ten students. You can audit it as the eleventh."

"I'd love to be in your seminar," she stammered, inordinately pleased.

"Think about applying for a scholarship. A degree is always a plus." Dr. Fletcher stood up. "Lovely day, isn't it? Think I'll get a cup of coffee at the bookstore. Want to come along?"

Annie's tongue thickened. What did she have to say to this woman that could possibly interest her? She'd look like a dope if she gave her opinion on anything.

In her moment of indecision, Jake Boyer happened upon them.

"There you are," he said. "I thought of something I forgot to ask. Hi, Annie."

"We're on our way to the bookstore for a coffee. Come with us." Annie tagged along, hanging back a little when there was no room for three on the sidewalk. Jake was talking. He had no trouble expressing himself in front of Fletcher. There was no awe in his voice or actions.

They walked down the narrow alley to the back door. Behind the counter stood a girl with spiked multicolored hair and rings in her nose, lower lip, and up and down her ears. Her exposed midriff, bared between tight pants and short top, showed off a pierced navel.

"Hey, girlfriend," Jake said cheerfully. "How's it going?"

"Good. There's a meeting tonight, you know."

"I'll be there to cover it," he promised.

Annie studied the short menu. She seldom ate out or went to the grocery store. Instead, she lived on leftover food from the restaurant.

"I'm treating," Dr. Fletcher said. "How about soup and bagels all around with coffee?"

They carried the food to a large table. Annie faced Dr. Fletcher and Jake.

"What are you reading?" Fletcher asked Annie.

"*The Caveman's Valentine.*"

"The one about the crazy homeless guy?" Jake said. "They made it into a movie."

"I'm not sure how crazy he is. He pulls himself together when he has to."

"I haven't read that one," Fletcher said.

"It's a murder mystery," Annie told her. "You probably wouldn't like it." She was sure Fletcher read only classics interspersed with National Book Award choices and books by Pulitzer and Nobel prize winners.

"I love mysteries. They're good fodder when you want to relax."

"My aunt reads them at night when she can't sleep," she said.

"Is that your real stepfather you write about?" Jake asked.

158

"Sometimes," Annie admitted. The stories were supposed to be fiction.

"You can fictionalize life. Most good writers do," Fletcher said. She motioned a couple of colleagues over to their table and introduced them to Annie and Jake.

"Dr. Daniels teaches American Writers and Dr. Judson specializes in English Literature. Why don't you join us?"

Annie and Jake wolfed down their soup and bagels and coffees, and excused themselves. Their leavetaking went hardly noticed, the three professors were so deep in conversation. A dialogue Annie was not qualified to participate in.

She and Jake went out the back door into the warm embrace of September. Before they parted at the next street, he for the campus, she for her rooming house, he said, "Don't forget to bring something to submit to the magazine."

High on Fletcher's and Boyer's affirmation of her writing, she bounded up the steps to her apartment. A large room with a bed in one corner, a kitchenette in another. A small bathroom with a new shower stall adjoined the room across the hall. Radiators provided heat. She'd splurged on a fan that gave the illusion of cooling by moving air around.

Changing clothes, she clambered down the stairs and rode the scooter to the restaurant a few blocks away, a college hangout that sold mostly sandwiches, burgers, fries, and salads. The tips were not good, the wages minimum. She barely made enough to pay the rent. She'd have to look for a better job if she wanted to continue auditing classes. She'd forgotten to ask the cost of the seminar.

When she helped close up around nine, her head was so filled with what she would say to Molly that she saw nothing on the way home.

Molly looked up from the small table where they ate and worked. "I can hardly stay awake, this text is so boring."

Kissing Molly hard on the mouth, she said, "Hungry? I brought some stuff from the restaurant."

"I ate at the dorm, but I'll have a little something."

159

In the end, they both ate a sandwich, salad, chips, and a piece of cake. There were only two hard rolls left over for breakfast and lunch.

She told Molly about Fletcher and Jake. "She treated us to lunch, and he wants me to submit a story to *The Campus Review*."

"You should be a student and have to read all this garbage. Then you wouldn't have so much time to write," Molly griped.

Stung, Annie said, "I'd still write. Dr. Fletcher said I should apply for a scholarship."

"You audit one class. You don't even have to worry about a grade. While I'm slaving over these boring books and going to these mind-numbing classes, you're having a good old time."

"Why don't you take something you like? You do have some choices."

"I know." Molly leaned back in the straight chair. She looked tired.

"I thought you were into economics and political science."

"I am."

Annie leaned forward. "What do you want to do?"

"I don't know," Molly said. "Let's go to bed for a while." Which was what they did when they tired of studying or, in Annie's case, writing. It gave them a pleasant break.

Molly fell asleep afterwards, nude, spread-eagled on the rumpled sheets, her skin still golden from days in the summer sun.

Pulling a sheet over Molly, Annie put on a T-shirt and shorts. She heated water for a cup of tea and sat at the table, contemplating her short story for the magazine. Traffic flowed on the street below her windows; voices drifted up and in through the screens.

She wrote on Molly's laptop. The story told of a gay man and the straight woman who was married to him.

When she returned to bed at two in the morning, the street below was as silent as the rest of the house. Molly turned away from her, curling into a ball, and Annie fitted her own body into her curves.

XXI
Josey

Josey gave up all efforts to work by mid-morning. Every time the phone rang, her heart leapt into high gear and calmed down only when the caller wasn't from the doctor's office.

At noon Ellen showed up with lunch. "Heard anything yet?"

Josey shook her head. "What's for lunch? Smells good."

"Broccoli soup and bagels."

Josey called, "Mary, Ellen's here."

"Shelley showed up at my door after midnight," Ellen said. "She stayed till morning."

"What's going on?" Mary asked, taking a sip. "The soup's wonderful. You made it?"

"Yep," Ellen said. "Tom was holed up with someone in the maintenance garage. The door was locked, so she hid around the corner until someone drove out. In a Ford extended-cab pickup."

Roy drove such a truck. Josey's mouth fell open with surprise.

When Ellen left, Mary said what Josey had been thinking, "Tom and Roy?"

Josey played devil's advocate. "Maybe it wasn't Roy. There are other pickups like his. Or maybe they were working on his pickup. They're friends."

"The fucker."

"If it's true, Tom isn't exactly an innocent party. A grown man with five sons." Josey laughed. "I thought lesbians were the athletes, not gay men."

"It's not funny, Josey." Mary looked grim.

"Not for Shelley," she agreed. "Not for Tom either." He'd lose his kids and Shelley. And she had no doubt a way would be found to force him out of his job.

She phoned the plastic surgeon's office at three, when Mary said, "I don't know about you, but I can't wait any longer."

On hold for Lieberman's assistant, Josey felt her heartbeat fill her head. Please, please, please.

A woman came on the line. Josey asked about the biopsy. "Let me look," the woman said. In a few moments she was back. "Good news."

Josey missed most of what else she said. Swamped with gratitude, her smile shaky, she admitted, "I was so afraid."

"Me too." Mary nodded at the phone. "You better call Ellen."

The relief evident in Ellen's voice prompted Josey to ask, "Coming over tonight to celebrate?"

"You bet."

"Bring your nightie." Josey hung up and walked to the windows, pushed open to admit any stray breeze. She felt an enormous appreciation for life. Mary came up behind her and put a hand on her shoulder.

They stood quietly for a few moments, looking at the millpond. Then Mary said, "Your turn to work. I'll stay out here."

As she drove home under threatening clouds, the benign biopsy report honed Josey's appreciation for her surroundings, bringing them into keen focus—images sharper, smells sweeter, sounds clearer. There were no decisions regarding chemotherapy or radiation treatments looming in the future, no drugs like tamoxifen. She felt as if she'd escaped something that might have been worse than dying. She only guessed why she hadn't fully appreciated this earlier. Perhaps she'd been in shock; everything had happened so quickly.

Roy was leaning against his truck, smoking. Parking next to it, she got out and opened the back to get the groceries she'd bought before leaving town. He put out his cigarette, took the bags from her, and carried them toward the house.

"I've got to talk to you."

"I don't want to hear it," she said, trying to pry the bags from him.

"You know what it's like." He threw her a pleading look.

"You and Tom?" she asked.

"We go back to high school. He's the only guy I ever loved."

"He's got five kids and a wife, who just happens to be a friend of yours. How could you?"

"I'll talk to Shelley."

"That's a terrific idea. Are you going to ask her to share her husband?"

He shrugged broad shoulders and gave her a rueful smile. "Scratch that. I'd have to talk to Tom first anyway."

"He was such a jock," Josey said. "The jocks are supposed to be the dykes."

Roy laughed. "Don't I know it. Those muscles made my heart throb. I've got almost as much claim on him as Shelley."

"He'd have to leave town."

"I'd leave, too. We could live together, finally."

"Do you want that?" She stared at him angrily, her own joy in the biopsy results forgotten.

"No, I suppose not. You can't build something on so much guilt, can you?"

"I don't know." She'd never given much thought to Tom Barnes. She pictured Tom passing a ball into the end zone, and Shelley doing her cheerleader routine. It must seem to Shelley that her life lay in shreds around her.

"How is Shelley?"

"She thinks another woman is the problem."

"Is it worse if it's a man?" he asked, setting the bags on the counter in the kitchen. He leaned over to pat Buddy.

"A woman she can deal with on an equal level. A man is another thing altogether. She can't change Tom if he's gay."

The dog ran to the door, welcoming Mary.

Mary studied Roy, her dark eyes snapping. "You son of a bitch."

He put his hands up as if surrendering. "I'm out of here."

When the door closed behind him, Mary asked, "What was he doing here?"

"Confessing. He and Tom go back to high school. He loves the man."

Mary looked astonished. "Who was that guy I caught him in bed with then?"

Josey shrugged. "A little indiscretion perhaps. You'll have to ask him."

When Ellen drove in, Mary and Josey had popped the cork on a bottle of wine and were working on dinner.

"I saw Roy on the road," Ellen said.

"He lives in Barkins Woods," Josey said. "That's not far."

"Anything I can do to help?"

"Let's toast first," Mary said, pouring the wine and lifting hers. "To Josey."

"Yeah, to me." She grinned, once again ebullient.

Later, Josey slid a hand into the V-neck of Ellen's shorty pajamas. The bedroom was warm, the windows cracked against rain coming down in torrents. Buddy lay panting on the floor.

"You're not up to this," Ellen said.

"I only want to touch."

"Touch all you want." Ellen met Josey's eyes.

"What do you think about us?"

"I think we better go slow here. I'm a little wary," Ellen replied.

"As you should be. I'm ashamed. I treated you badly."

"It was a bad time."

"I envy you your clear eyes. You always look like you sleep well."

"I usually do."

"And you always speak in perfect prose, not like the rest of us."

Ellen laughed. "If you're trying to win me over, you're wasting your time. You already have."

On the way to the Mill the next day, Josey pulled over on the sandy berm.

"Something wrong?" Ellen called, getting out of her car.

"Nope. I'm just picking some of these asters to put on the counter in the shop. They're the color of your eyes." She took the penknife on her key chain and cut the stems, careful not to pull them out of the ground.

"You're like a different person, Josey," Ellen said, clipping the wildflowers herself.

"It won't last. Mary says I'm a cynic. But all that garbage about life being too short to not live fully is true. And embarrassingly trite to say aloud." She straightened.

Ellen squinted at Josey, one hand clutching the asters and some small white flowers. "You've just found out how mortal you are."

She held Ellen's gaze for a moment. "Yes, I have." For the first time since the mastectomy, she felt lucky.

XXII
Annie

She'd been prepared to read the story in class on Thursday, but Fletcher hadn't called on her. So she turned it in for Fletcher to read before giving it to Jake. It was very short and began with a description of Josey as she'd first seen her.

"Do you have anything for the magazine?" Jake asked as she slung her backpack over one shoulder after class.

"I handed it in. You can have it next week if Fletcher thinks it's okay. I don't want to give you a piece of crap."

"You'd know if it was," he told her. "Want to go get coffee or a bagel or something?"

"Sure." There was no place she had to be.

"Why aren't you a student?" he asked. The day was cool, gray. Students flowed around them on either side.

She told him the truth as she'd told Fletcher. She shivered a little in the damp air.

"It was in the papers and on TV, wasn't it?" he said, looking at her curiously. "I remember thinking I'd probably have been there myself. So they threw you out?"

"Yep. Took away my scholarship. I turned twenty-one this summer, a couple months too late, but maybe that wouldn't have made any difference." She was happy to be here anyway, glad to have met Molly.

The bookstore smelled of coffee. The same girl stood behind the counter, dressed in practically the same garb.

"Is she a student?" she asked when she and Jake took a seat in the back room.

"Yep. She belongs to the GLBT group. I cover most of the clubs on campus for the *Review*."

Annie hadn't gotten any vibes, but maybe she wasn't tuned in. She preferred a more conventional look. "She looks like she was shot full of holes," she whispered.

He laughed and fingered the small ring in his ear. "Better than a tattoo. The holes heal over when you're done with them, or at least you can't see them."

The door opened and they both looked up. The two professors who had joined them when they had lunch with Fletcher nodded in their direction and headed toward the counter.

"Have you read Fletcher's books of short stories?" he asked.

"No," she said.

"I've got them. Would you like to borrow them?"

"Would I ever," she said.

"Where do you live? I'll bring them over."

She heard their voices as she unlocked the door after work. Under the fly-specked globe over the table, Molly and Jake stopped talking, their eyes on her. She hadn't forgotten the books of short stories he'd promised to lend her, but it wasn't until he held up the two thin volumes that she realized why he was there.

Taking them, she studied the covers and flipped through the pages. "Thanks. I'll read them right away."

"No rush," he said.

"Do you two know each other?" she asked. They looked so comfortable together.

"We do now," Molly replied. "What do you think, Annie? Are we the only reality?"

"You mean, if a tree falls in the woods, does it make any sound if no one's around? The laws of physics say it does." Actually, she knew nothing about physics. She emptied her backpack, dumping the styrofoam containers from the restaurant onto the table, and shrugged out of her jacket.

"Dinner," she said to Boyer's upraised brows.

"You always eat this late?"

"I don't turn down free meals."

"I should go," Jake said, pushing himself to his feet. "I've got work to do."

"See you next week," Annie said.

"Want to go out for fish Friday night?" he asked.

The two young women looked at each other and him, not sure whom he was asking.

"Both of you."

"What time?" Molly askedd.

"I have to work," Annie said. She couldn't afford meals out anyway.

When they no longer heard his steps on the stairs, Annie spoke. "You're going out on a date, huh?"

"I'm going out for fish. He's editor of the *Review* and a big man on campus, Annie. You're going to publish your stories because of him."

"And what are you going to get out of him?" Annie asked nastily.

"I'll meet people. The more contacts the better."

"Opportunist," Annie muttered.

"Aren't we all," Molly agreed. "It's who you know that pays off sometimes."

"I guess. I choose my friends for something other than what they can do for me." She paged through one of Fletcher's books, not seeing past the blur of print.

Molly tossed her head. "Don't you go out for coffee with him?"

Why were they carping at each other? She told herself to shut up, to not make it any worse. Why shouldn't Molly go out for supper with Boyer?

"You want me to sleep at the dorm tonight?" Molly snapped.

Annie looked at Molly, saw her eyes dark with anger. "I'm sorry," she said. "Let's just go to bed."

"You're a jealous woman." A smile lifted the corners of Molly's mouth, but failed to reach her eyes.

Annie undressed, watching Molly throw off her shirt and sweatpants. It still moved her when Molly gave herself, but tonight Molly pulled the sheet up to her chin and turned her back.

After a while, Annie got up, padded over to the one chair under the cheap floor lamp, and opened the first book of Fletcher's short stories. She read from cover to cover. She loved the characters, their unconventional lives and attitudes—mostly poor women braving their way through their days and nights. Toughened by dysfunctional childhoods, difficult marriages, hardscrabble jobs, they refused to be compromised.

She sat under the low glow of the lamp, the book closed in her lap. Exhaustion flowed through her, but she could sleep till it was time to go to work. Finally, she climbed back in bed with Molly. When the people in the books stopped traipsing through her thoughts, she fell asleep.

Awakening shortly after ten in the morning to an empty flat, she got up and looked for a note. Finding none, she made herself coffee and returned to bed with the other book of short stories.

Rain tapped against the windows. She hunkered down under the blankets, occasionally getting up to eat something—a bowl of cereal, peanut butter on toast. She was still hungry when she got ready for work.

The rain stopped and she went outside, her hair shower wet. Unlocking the scooter from the porch post, she bumped it down the steps and purred off through the mist toward the restaurant.

Friday came, throwing Annie into a fit of angst as she watched Molly change outfits. "Why are you trying to impress him?" She herself was getting ready for work.

"I'm not, stupid. I always change clothes before I go out. Don't you?"

"I don't try on dozens of clothes." Certainly not for some man. "Where are you going? Maybe I'll come over afterwards. Or you could come to the restaurant and I could wait on you. Their fish fry's not bad."

Molly ended up in jeans and a plaid shirt. "How do I look?" She turned in a slow circle.

"Goddamn gorgeous. He's going to come on to you."

"Forget it. He's not even cute." Molly looked exasperated. "I don't know where we're going. Maybe we'll stop in and see you."

"Yeah, do that," Annie said.

Molly gave her a light kiss. "Otherwise, I'll see you in bed."

Jake and Molly didn't stop at the restaurant where Annie worked. Molly wasn't at the apartment either. Annie flopped in the lone chair and opened Fletcher's book, but her mind wandered. At eleven she went outside to walk the streets in a cold wind.

She hurried past the warm lights of campus housing on her way to the river at the bottom of a long hill. Laughter and music and people moving behind the windows reached inside her to the lonely spot that only Molly filled.

Tired and cold, she stood on the bridge over the dark water.

Leaning on the railing, watching the steaming surface, she felt as bleak as the river looked.

She turned toward her flat, head down, hands stuffed in pockets, and suddenly in a hurry, strode toward home. Light leaked out from under the door, and Annie unlocked it and entered quietly, her eyes immediately honing in on the bed.

She hadn't realized she'd been holding her breath until she exhaled in relief. Molly lay alone, curled fetus-like in sleep. Quietly removing her clothes, she slipped into the warm bed and shivered for a few minutes, then wrapped herself around Molly, drawing heat from her.

"Where were you?" Molly murmured sleepily.

"Out. Where were you?"

"We went to Boyer's frat house after dinner. It's over by the river."

She'd probably passed under its windows while Molly was there. "What did you do?"

"Talked. Studied."

Annie phoned her mother from a pay phone on campus over the weekend. She told her that Fletcher had invited her to audit her seminar.

"Have you called about your suspension?"

"I don't want to go back there. I'm learning more here."

"We can't afford the tuition there."

"I know, Mom. When am I going to see you?"

"I'll come next Saturday. I'm not scheduled to work."

Afraid she'd have to explain Molly, she said impulsively, "I'll take that night off. We can go to Josey's, if she's not doing anything."

"I'll call Josey," her mother said.

"I haven't seen the twins since I left, and I've only seen Jeanne once. Think they would come?"

"If they can. I miss you, sweetie."

"Me, too."

XXIII
Josey

She'd almost finished the *Woman in the Mirror* series, and Mary was after her to hang two of the paintings on the wall at the Mill. "Too personal," she said, crossing her arms to brace herself against Mary's persuasiveness.

They were having lunch with Ellen, who said, "I talked to my friend who runs a gallery in Appleton. She's always got a show going. I told her you didn't want the paintings to go to a private party."

"That's better than putting them on the wall here. More exposure," Mary said excitedly.

"I don't want exposure," Josey protested. "Not with those paintings."

"Only with exposure do you become really successful, Jose," Mary said patiently, as if she were talking to a child.

"That's not why I painted them, Mare," she shot back. "They were therapy. Now the sessions are almost over and the subject can be put to rest."

Mary heaved a great sigh. "No one's going to connect you personally to these paintings."

"But she would be expected to be there opening night," Ellen said.

"You go for me, Mary, and I'll exhibit."

Mary said firmly, "I'll go with you."

"And so will I," Ellen put in.

Fall was everywhere—in the nutty smell of woods, the yellowing of grass, the fading crimson of the poison sumac, the wilting asters, the red and yellow maples, the brownish red oak leaves. She drove home in a haze of dust that hung over everything.

Roy's truck hunkered in the driveway. She found him on the front porch, sitting in one of the chairs, feet on the railing, a cigarette in hand. He offered her the open pack.

"Let's have a drink with it," she said, the surprise of his unexpected presence already gone.

His feet dropped to the porch floor. "I was hoping you'd say that." He followed her to the kitchen. "I'll have a beer."

She heard it in his careful pronunciation. "You've had a head start, haven't you?"

"Yep. Tom dumped me before I could dump him. He doesn't want to lose his kids." He popped the tab and took a long swig. She mixed herself a vodka and tonic.

"Come on, let's go outside and have that smoke."

"He'll go elsewhere. I just hope he's careful." Roy settled back in the porch chair and crossed his feet on the railing.

"You'll find someone else."

"Easy for you to say. You've got Ellen," he said enviously.

"Everything's not coming up roses there either," she said after a moment of silence. A symphony of crickets sawed in the tall grass.

"No?" he said, bending over to look into her face. "Why not?"

She turned her head away, wondering why she was confiding in him. "Forget I said that. I love Ellen. I do." Although theirs was becoming more of a friendship than anything else, she thought. They spent their evenings as if they'd been together for years—playing scrabble or cribbage, reading, watching a program on TV or a video, talking, going to bed around nine to read some more or, infrequently, to make love. Friendship should be the basis of any relationship, she reasoned. At her age, why would she expect red-hot passion?

"For chrissake," he said. "Why does everything have to be so complicated?"

"Because people are complex," she said.

He leaned back. "Listen to those little buggers. First it's the frogs, then it's the birds, now it's the crickets. Do you think they're courting?"

"I suppose," she said.

"Everyone but me is getting it." He sighed.

She ground out her cigarette and put it in a crock near the door as Ellen drove in.

"Got to go now, sweetheart. How's Mary?"

"She's got a manfriend," she blurted.

"I know. I'm glad for her." But he sounded sad.

Roy stopped to exchange a greeting with Ellen on the way to his truck. Josey hurried inside to brush her teeth and down the rest of the drink, hoping to dispel the smell of the cigarette.

Glad that Ellen had dug in her heels about living together, yet in no hurry to end their liaison, she hoped that, given time, things would sort themselves out. She returned to the kitchen as Ellen set a bottle of wine on the table.

"I talked with Jewel on the phone about dates," Ellen said.

"No hello, how are you?" Josey kissed her on the cheek.

174

"I just saw you at noon." Ellen turned her head so that her lips met Josey's.

"When is this exhibit?"

"Mid-October. Two weeks after your reconstruction. Will you be up to it?"

"Can I use that as an excuse?" Did she want to? Now that she had agreed to display the paintings, she was curious as to how people would react.

Ellen shrugged. "I suppose you could."

"Mary's not going to let me hide forever. I may as well get it over with."

"What did Roy have to say?"

Josey thought guiltily of her admission that her relationship with Ellen lacked excitement and passion. "We had a drink together. Tom dumped him."

Josey had briefly met Terry MacMillan, Mary's love interest, a quiet man with a smile that warmed his eyes. When he walked into the Mill the next day, she would have failed to recognize him had he not stuck out a hand, big and reddened by weather.

"Hi. Remember me? Mac?"

Josey pictured him in a boat, checking fishing licenses, or tread through public woods and fields, making sure hunters wore blaze orange with their number fastened on the back. Actually, Mary said he spent much of his time at a computer. "Sure do. Mary's in the back room, hard at work." She gestured toward the workshop.

She really was glad for Mary, but this guy she thought was much too young. He was no doubt enamored of Mary's beauty. When it faded, there were always her strong personality, her enormous talent, her brains and wit. Any man would be lucky to be chosen by her.

The door opened with a jangle as Candy's and John's mothers came in. Reenie and Brenda. "Are you out browsing?"

"John asked me to look you up, actually. He wants to know how to get hold of your niece," Brenda said.

"She has no phone. Why don't you give me John's number, so she can call him?" As Brenda wrote down the information, Josey asked, "How are John and Candy?"

"Candy's abandoned us," Reenie said. "She loves Ripon."

"John hasn't been home much either," Brenda added, then asked, "Are you still doing horse portraits, because we wondered if you'd like to have a booth at the horse fair in Oshkosh in March?"

"You bet," she said without asking how much. "Got any literature?"

"Only last year's." They spread it out on the counter. "It's twelve hundred fifty for a ten-by-ten space."

"I could get by with half of that," Josey said. One portrait commission would pay for it.

"We'll put you on the list and get back with you," Brenda said as they left.

Mary and Mac walked out of the workshop, his arm steering her toward the door. "We're going out for a while," Mary said, her cheeks red, her eyes bright.

Josey didn't ask where. She knew and envied them their passion.

The weekend with Annie, her mother, and her other nieces pleased Josey. As they left, she stood with Buddy among the sparse grass, a hand lifted in farewell, a feeling of loneliness creeping over her. She should have been glad to reclaim her solitude and would have been, she realized, if just one of them had stayed behind.

Annie had talked about her writing, had mentioned the story that she'd been asked to submit to the *Review*. Watching her, Josey realized how much this meant to her niece. She remembered herself as a young woman wanting only to paint.

"Want to go for a walk, Buddy?"

At the word "walk" Buddy raced in tight circles, making her

laugh, and she started down the path to the trout pond. The dog quickly caught up and passed her, legs reaching, belly barely clearing the ground, tongue hanging out, ears flat. The streamlined look, she thought with amusement.

Burnished by the sun, surrounded by yellowing aspens, the pond's still surface was broken by a small fleet of mallards, two mergansers, and a lone loon. The loon she saw only in spring and fall as it migrated through. Its eerie call punctuated the gabbling of the ducks. The merganzers would leave when the edges of the pond began to freeze, putting them at risk of predation. The mallards sometimes stayed into the winter, though, treading the open current.

Flies lazed around her head and she waved her hat to keep them away. Cross-legged, she sat in the sand and squinted at the sunlight on the pond. Buddy climbed into her lap and licked her face, but she hardly noticed.

As she had before, she told herself that she was lucky to have Ellen. Ellen was smart, kind, shared her politics, her love of reading. She should be ashamed complaining to Roy about the missing passion. But she'd seen Mary and Mac's eagerness to bed each other and knew she'd never felt that way about Ellen and probably never would. It saddened her, but there it was.

She should be thankful, and she was. She thought she'd come to terms with dying, yet now when life spread before her, the years ahead were not enough to satisfy her.

"I'm not a grateful person, doggy. I want too much. Just like everyone else, I'm selfish and greedy." She stretched her head back as Buddy lapped at her chin.

Ellen phoned, as she'd promised she would, to say she was back from La Crosse, and did Josey want to come over and spend the night. She was making homemade pizza.

Loading Buddy into the car, she drove slowly, on the lookout for deer made jittery by the bow and arrow season. Parking in Ellen's driveway, she released Buddy into the fenced-in yard and entered the kitchen through the patio doors.

Ellen wore an apron over her shorts and T-shirt and was deftly slicing onions, arranging them on the pizza crust along with bits of broccoli.

"Anything I can do to help?" Josey asked.

"Sure. Pop the cork on the wine. I'm pining for a glass." Only Ellen said such things.

Josey smiled. "Have you ever tried writing poetry?"

"Trust me. I have no talent for poetry." She slugged back the wine as soon as Josey poured it.

"What is it?" She'd never seen Ellen gulp her alcohol.

"I'm working up some courage here." Ellen shot her a dark blue look.

Josey downed her glass. "In that case, maybe I better swallow some too." She washed her hands and began shredding cheese as, with mixed feelings, she waited to hear what Ellen had to say. Her heart thumped a little faster in anticipation. "Spit it out," she demanded.

Wiping her hands on the apron, Ellen said, "Let me get this in the oven first. Then we'll go out on the deck with our wine."

Once on the deck, though, Ellen refilled their glasses and sipped hers as if in deep thought.

"Ellen, come on. Share. You've got me worried."

Turning in Josey's direction, Ellen said, "Hear me out, Josey. Then you can talk."

"All right," she agreed.

"You know that Bonnie Raitt song, 'I can't make you love me if you don't'?" Josey nodded and Ellen plunged on. "I've always known that my feelings toward you are stronger than yours toward me."

Josey opened her mouth to protest, but Ellen stopped her with a hand up. "I know you love me as a friend; we'll always be friends." Ellen tucked her lower lip between her teeth, something she did when thinking. "We could make a stab at living together. We have like interests, like minds. They make up the glue of a relationship, but maybe you need the passion first. Anyway, something's missing." Ellen blinked, and Josey put a hand over hers.

"What's wrong with trying?" she asked.

"I've been offered a really good job in La Crosse, too good to turn down at this stage of my life."

"Oh," Josey said. "Well, I don't want to stand in the way." She tried to look into Ellen's eyes, but Ellen averted her face. "When would you go?"

"Not till the beginning of the year."

"Maybe I can change your mind."

"Maybe you would come with me," Ellen said, but both of them knew that wasn't an option for Josey. Her home, her business, her roots were here. She'd said so more than once.

Josey tossed the wine down her throat and poured them both more. She felt immeasurably sad, but along with the sadness came a sense of relief, and a little excitement at being set free.

XXIV
Annie

Over the weekend, Annie vowed to let Molly go without a scene, although she knew it would hurt terribly. She'd say nothing if she went out with Jake, even slept with him, unless she was tacky enough to do it in Annie's bed.

She was ready to talk, and there was no one to talk to. Her aunt spent most of the weekend with Annie's mother. Annie showed her sisters around. There was no opportunity to be alone with Josey. Besides, she was sure her aunt had never felt the despair she suspected was waiting for her when Molly did leave.

She knew no one on campus besides Molly and Jake and Dr. Fletcher. Envisioning the lonely days and nights, she felt defeated by them, and desperate.

When Annie let herself into the flat after her mother dropped her off, her heart lifted at the sight of Molly, then fell upon seeing Jake. Both sat at the paper-strewn table, bent over textbooks.

"How was Clover?" Molly asked.

"Don't know. We didn't go into town."

"Annie's aunt is an artist. She and a friend run the Pottery and Art Mill in Clover."

"Talent runs in the family, I guess," Jake said.

It was hard to dislike him when he said things like that. "I've got to change and go to work." Annie wondered if they'd used the bed yet, if she'd have to sleep on their spent passion. It drove her crazy thinking that way, but her mind wouldn't let it alone.

"I have to go to a meeting." Jake stood up and gathered his things. "See you in Fletcher's class, Annie, and you tomorrow night, Moll."

"What's tomorrow night?" Annie asked with pretended casualness when he was gone.

"We're going to study at the frat house. He's helping me with a paper I'm writing."

"Oh," Annie replied, stifling the urge to tell her she could help her. Molly surely knew that. She pulled a clean shirt over her head and sucked in air sharply when she felt Molly's hands on her breasts.

"Got a few minutes?" Molly asked with a sly grin as Annie turned in her arms to face her.

"Later," Annie said.

"Not even for a quickie?" Molly persisted, unzipping Annie's jeans and slipping her hand under the elastic of her panties.

They were good at quickies. Annie shed her shirt, stepped out of her jeans and undies and helped Molly undress. They fell on the bed in a tangle of limbs, lips bruising, tongues searching, and stroked each other to climax in record time.

"I've got to go now," Annie breathed into Molly's mouth.

Molly rolled away with a small, satisfied smile. "All right."

"Will you be here when I get home?"

"Yes. I've got a couple of exams tomorrow."

❧

Annie slid down in her seat when Fletcher singled out her short story to read. Sure that everyone would guess she was gay, Annie felt as if her eyes were burning holes in her flushed face. Why else would she write about a gay man?

Sarah looked up from the rows of vegetables, clumps of weeds in one hand, as George drove in. She straightened, one hand in the small of her back, and shielded her eyes from the morning sun peering over the treetops. A few stray hairs swirled around her face in the warm breeze.

She wondered what excuse he'd have this time and waited, steeling herself against doubt as he strode to the edge of the garden.

"Would you believe I fell asleep in the truck?" He stuffed his hands in his back pockets and kicked at the sandy soil. "No?"

She shook her head, now girding herself against the truth.

His sigh told her he'd decided to tell her what she already knew, that he was cheating on her. "I met someone. I spent the night with him." He looked away, avoiding her eyes.

Shock rippled through her. She'd known, of course, deep down where she hid what she didn't want to admit to herself. She stared at his face for a few minutes, as if trying to memorize it for one of her paintings. She'd always thought him beautiful.

He stretched out a hand placatingly, and she looked at it as if it were a foreign object. "I'm sorry."

"Why did you marry me?" she asked flatly to hide the pain. A slight quaver gave it away.

He shrugged. "I love you. Do you think we can live with this?"

Anger flared in her. "Is it a one-time thing?"

"All I know is I don't want to move out."

"You want a lot." She looked at the blue bowl of sky dotted with pink clouds and heard the cardinal singing in the maple tree. Taking a deep breath, she smelled the fresh morning air and turned her gaze on the bunches of daisies growing untamed in the yard. It only felt like the end of everything she loved. She'd survive . . .

Fletcher stopped reading and asked the class for comments.

"It grabs your attention right away," one of the guys said.

"Good characterization," a girl added, "and excellent descriptions. I could see everything—the two people, the garden, the sky, the flowers. And I felt her sense of betrayal."

That was what she herself was feeling with Molly, Annie thought, waiting for Jake to comment. She felt his eyes on her and met them, seeing the vaguely puzzled look.

"Anyone else?" Fletcher asked.

There were other remarks, almost all of them laudatory, until one of the guys who sat in the front of the class said, "I'd like to know what Miss Spitz is trying to say."

Fletcher raised her eyebrows at Annie, who went on the defensive. "The story's about infidelity and what it does to a person." She thought that was pretty obvious.

"Why does the guy have to be gay?" the young man asked, turning to look at Annie.

"Why does he have to be straight?" she shot back. "Actually, though, it's harder if he's gay, because then Sarah can't really win him back."

"Short stories are often slices of life," Dr. Fletcher said, taking control again. "This is a good portrayal of a relationship in crisis that, as Miss Spitz said, can't be satisfactorily resolved."

Annie felt some of the color drain from her face, leaving her layered in sweat. Jake, who usually took an active part in any critiques, still said nothing. He was looking straight ahead now, and she wondered if he would print this story.

Fletcher didn't read whatever Jake had written, instead reading from stories by students less frequently chosen.

After class, Jake put a hand out for the story that Fletcher had passed back to Annie. "I'll try," he said. "The faculty editor is a little rigid."

She handed the folder to him with a tight smile. "I can always write another." Out of the corner of her eye, she caught Fletcher beckoning to them as she and Jake headed toward the door.

When the other students wandered away, Fletcher said, "Your story was well written, Mr. Boyer, as you can see from my comments. Which to read was a toss-up. I chose Ms. Spitz's because of its novelty. I wanted to force the class to venture into new territory, to explore a little."

Jake brightened under Fletcher's praise. Annie wondered if he'd been upset not with the content of her story but because Fletcher hadn't read his stuff. "Are you two off to get coffee? If you are, I'll walk with you."

If they weren't before, they were now, Annie thought. She looked into Fletcher's eyes briefly and saw the steel softened with a smile. "I'm meeting my colleagues at the bookstore, and I have a few things I want to talk to you two about."

They waded through leaves as they walked across campus. Fletcher said, "I'm putting together an anthology of students' stories, with their written permission of course. I need someone to read the stories first and send the best on to me. Are either or both of you interested?"

Annie jumped at the offer without questions. "I am."

"What about you, Mr. Boyer? There is a stipend that goes with this job. Eight dollars an hour. You keep track of your time."

"I'd like, no, I'd love to, but I'm so snowed under." It was the first time Annie heard him stammer. "When would you want us to start?"

"Don't do it if it's going to jeopardize your other classes or your work on the *Review*."

Annie walked lightly, her feet floating, not slogging, through the leaves. Eight bucks an hour. Maybe she could quit her job. She had applications elsewhere, none of which had come through yet. "I'll start right now," she said.

Fletcher laughed. "Good girl." She put a hand on Annie's shoulder, imprinting her light touch in the girl's mind. "Come to my office tomorrow at nine. I'll give you a batch to start you off."

They were at the back door of the bookstore, and Jake opened and held it for them. Inside, Fletcher's two colleagues were seated at the largest table. She stopped to greet them, and Annie and Jake went to the counter to order. He asked for tuna on a bagel and coffee, and she splurged on a bagel with cream cheese and coffee. It felt like a celebration of sorts.

Fletcher came to the counter as they paid. They took their food and drinks to a small table along the wall, politely greeting Fletcher's professional friends on their way.

"You and Molly are pretty close," Jake said before he put his mouth around the sandwich.

"I guess," she replied with a shrug that pretended indifference, and changed the subject. "You didn't comment on my story."

He swallowed, his Adam's apple bobbing in his thick neck. "I know. I would have said what the others said, except for that jerk in the front row."

"Are you really going to have trouble getting it in the *Review*?" she asked.

"I was just pissed because Fletcher didn't read mine," he said quietly, throwing a glance at the professors, who were deep in conversation.

"Can I read yours?" she asked, liking and hating him at the same time. If Molly was fucking him, she'd picked a nice guy to do it with, almost as nice as John Lovelace. She had called John yesterday from a pay phone; he only had a few minutes to talk; but they agreed to get together when next they were both in the same place.

"Sure, but I'm putting it in the magazine. You can read it then. I don't want to bore you."

When they left, the professors never saw them go, so engaged with what they had to say to each other.

"I've got a question. You can tell me to shove it if you want. Don't feel you have to answer. Why are you here? Just to audit one class?"

Annie weighed her answer carefully, and lied. "Fletcher's class." She'd never heard of Fletcher, had only chosen to audit the class on a whim while leafing through a list of those offered. She'd followed Molly here, but she'd never admit that. Not only would it give away her sexual orientation and Molly's, but it would make her look like a camp follower or something weak like that.

"Fletcher's good, but I didn't know her reputation had spread to other places." As they passed a garbage bin, Jake tossed a discarded pop can into it. "Molly's always at your place."

"Not always," she said warily.

He grunted. "I gave her my frat pin. Did she tell you? I never had much use for it, to tell the truth, but you have to belong to get anywhere."

A white heat suffused her. "No. When?"

"Sunday."

Molly had come onto her Sunday. After she'd returned from work, they'd made long, slow love. She tried to find her way through a mess of conflicting feelings.

"You really care for her, don't you?" he asked.

"I guess," she said before her throat closed.

XXV
Josey

She met Jewel a week after the day the plastic surgeon took the bandages off, after which she and Ellen took the paintings to the gallery. In that week Josey had finished the third painting. The woman in the mirror had scars on both breasts, the one left by the mastectomy and reconstruction, the other a thin vertical line made in the healthy breast to tighten and raise it so that there was a semblance of balance between the two.

Jewel's long black hair was swept up and held flamboyantly in place by a turban, her neck and wrists encircled by gold chains, her ears sporting gold loops. She wore a brightly colored silken top and slacks.

After they left the gallery, they went to the restaurant where Annie worked, the College Drop In. The place was blue with cigarette smoke, so much that even Josey coughed. But they braved it in order to snatch a few minutes with Annie between customers.

The *Campus Review* had just come out, Annie told them, and handed a copy to Josey. "Look at it later. My story's in it." She smiled proudly.

Josey responded with a pleased smile of her own. "Thanks. I look forward to reading it."

"I do, too," Ellen said, then prompted, "Don't you have something to tell Annie, Josey?"

"I have a series of paintings on exhibit at The Jewel Gallery on the west end of town. Friday is opening night with a reception from seven to nine. Think you can get away? Mary and Ellen and I'll be there."

"I'll get away," Annie promised, "even if I have to quit this job."

"Don't do anything rash," Josey counseled. "It'll be on for a couple of weeks."

Annie slid into a chair at their table as they dug into their sandwiches and chips. "I've got another job." She told them about Fletcher's offer to pay her to read other people's stories. "She trusts me to pick out the best ones." For Ellen's benefit, she added, "Dr. Fletcher is the prof who asked me to be in her writing seminar next semester. I'm auditing her creative writing class."

"That's wonderful," Ellen said.

"Thanks. I'm excited about the art show, Josey. Really, I am." She spoke as if she were afraid she hadn't shown enough enthusiasm. Then another couple came through the door, and she left to take their orders.

Josey and Ellen finished their food and left a healthy tip. Outside, Josey breathed the chilly air to clear her lungs before climbing into Ellen's car. "I think I'm cured of cigarettes."

Glittering stars poked holes in the black sky. Josey lay her head on the back of the seat, anxious to get home. "Should I make it easier for her to follow Molly instead of going back to Madison?"

"What do you mean?" Ellen asked, her face lit briefly in an oncoming car's lights.

"I can't justify giving her money to stay here. She should be at the university." She snorted a laugh for thinking she had any money to spare. The medical bills were yet to come in for the reconstructive surgery.

"I agree with you. She'll find the right way more quickly if she spends her own money. You'd take her back in, though, wouldn't you, if she needed a place to stay?"

"In a minute."

On the Friday of the exhibit opening, Josey and Roy waited on Josey's porch for Mary and Ellen to drive in. Josey had changed clothes four times before settling on a pair of black slacks, a white shirt, and a vest. Her unruly gray-black hair curled around her ears. She and Roy climbed into the backseat of the Taurus.

Since Mary had met Mac, her anger toward Roy had faded into a thin veneer of sarcasm. She'd told Josey not long ago that what she missed most was the way Roy made her laugh. Mac was a more serious man.

Josey stared at the passing landscape. The hills of the county flattened in the next one. The woods turned into fields, the streams into sloughs, heading toward the Wolf River and its flowages. Closer to Appleton, urban sprawl took over the scenery. Tracts of immense houses sprang out of flatness with nothing to soften their starkness.

They took the north ramp onto Highway 41 and turned east onto College Avenue. Parking behind the gallery, they entered through the back door. Jewel was standing at a banquet table, talking to Annie. Both looked up as they entered.

"Annie is our server tonight," Jewel said.

"How . . . ?" Josey asked her niece, as Annie popped the cork on a bottle of champagne and poured the foaming liquid into glasses.

"I stopped in. She needed a server." Annie nodded toward Josey's paintings, highlighted by overhead track lighting. "I can't take my eyes off them."

"Did you quit your job?" Josey asked.

"I got someone to work for me. Who is the *Woman in the Mirror*?"

Mary accepted a glass and whispered something in Annie's ear. Annie dropped the question.

Others flowed in the back door, and Jewel took Josey's arm. "I want you to meet the rest of our artists."

The last thing Josey wanted was to talk about the *Woman in the Mirror*. She skillfully led any inquiries back to the artists' own works. Before long, though, she found herself standing in front of her own paintings, surrounded by others.

"You've caught the woman's emotions so well," one said.

"A good friend of mine," Josey murmured the lie.

Jewel rescued her, herding them all into a line near the entrance to meet the public. It was going to be a long night. Josey bolstered herself with a glass of wine. They had drunk the one bottle of champagne.

After a while, the artists drifted off one by one to mingle, she among them. She looked for Ellen and Mary and saw them in a far corner, conversing with one of the artists.

Ambling over to Annie, she held out her glass for Annie to fill and gazed at the crowd that had gathered. She knew no one but her friends, her niece, and Jewel. This would be a good time to network with other artists, to share techniques and marketing tips, if she could just avoid talking about her own set of paintings.

Annie startled her by asking, "It's not my mom in those pictures, is it?"

"Your mother? No, Annie. What made you think that?"

The girl shrugged. "I don't know. I haven't seen much of her. She might not tell me."

"She'd tell you," she said, not at all sure that was true. She took Annie's hand awkwardly and squeezed it. "It's not your mother."

Recalling Mary whispering in Annie's ear, Josey asked, "What did Mary say to you?"

"That she represented all women."

"She does." Those were the words she would use if asked.

Jewel was greeting two men and a woman at the door. Hearing Annie's quick intake of breath, she turned back to her.

"That's Dr. Fletcher and two of the other English professors. You've got to meet her, Josey," Annie whispered urgently, her face flushed, her voice animated.

"I'm sure Jewel will bring her over," Josey said. "First I need to connect with these other artists." Already she had forgotten their names.

Carrying her glass of wine, she crossed to the painting next to her series, memorized the artist's name, and waited for him to approach her. Artists were drawn to someone showing interest in their work. Several people crowded around her series, but she studiously ignored them. She had no interest in selling to a private party.

"There you are," Jewel's strident voice raised the hair on the back of her neck. "Stop hiding, Josey. Your series is the talk of the show."

"I'm not hiding. I wanted to exchange notes with some of the other artists." Where was the person who had slapped the paint on this canvas? She liked it. "Can you point this artist out to me? I want to talk to him."

"First, I want you to meet Dr. Lauren Fletcher, Dr. Michael Judson, and Dr. Hugh Daniels. They know your niece."

She found herself staring into Dr. Fletcher's gray blue eyes. The woman was as tall as she was, and imposing. "My niece, Annie, is auditing your creative writing class. She's excited about the reading job you've offered her."

"She's a good writer or I wouldn't have chosen her. What she's going to find out is that students' short stories aren't always stimulating."

Dr. Daniels stood with his hands behind his back. "This is your series, Ms. Duprey?"

She nodded and, as they shuffled over to stare at her work, Mary and Ellen converged on them. Moral support, she thought. She needed it.

When she made the introductions, she stepped back mentally and looked at each person. Mary, beautiful and talented. Ellen, cute and intelligent. The three professors had nothing on her friends, she told herself, despite their Ph.D.'s.

"What do you want for these paintings?" Daniels asked.

Fletcher leaned closer to the plaques. "They're not for sale. Is that right, Ms. Duprey?"

"That's right. Call me Josey."

Dressed in a ruby red outfit, gold in her ears and around her neck and wrists, Jewel fluttered over. "But if it were to go into a permanent public collection, perhaps Josey could be persuaded to sell."

"I'll send the head of the art department to take a look. He'll probably come anyway. You know him, Jewel? Bob Ruckman?"

"I do indeed know him, and he is coming to the exhibit, but not tonight."

Josey's gaze strayed to Lauren Fletcher. She was disconcerted to find Fletcher looking back. High cheekbones, a straight nose, and a strong jawline gave her a chiseled look. Her eyes were more blue than gray. An arched brow questioned Josey.

Mary moved in. "The series deserves an audience. It speaks to every woman." She gestured. "In the first painting the woman knows she is going to lose a breast; she's mourning. In the second, the breast is gone; the woman's feeling shock and horror. In the third, she's more or less restored even though both breasts are scarred. Her head is higher, but she knows now how vulnerable she is, how mortal."

Josey smiled faintly, silently applauding Mary.

"I shouldn't be talking for Josey," Mary said with a false modesty that made Josey want to laugh. "I'm just a potter."

"Are you?" Fletcher said. "I love pottery. I'll have to come to your place of business. Have you got a card?"

"I always carry some. Josey and I are in business together."

"Would you explain the colors, Josey?" Ellen urged.

She had thought the colors out carefully. Only the blue had been self-evident. "The red in the first painting signals a warning. The blue represents sadness, of course. In the third, the yellow symbolizes the sun, the sustainer of life." She shrugged away the drama she thought the words evoked. A little wine soaked and ego stroked, she floated on an artificial high.

Then she was tired of talking about her work and wanted to move on to others. She excused herself and walked away. Ellen and Mary remained behind.

Tired, having slept little the night before, she sat on a bench in the middle of the room. From that vantage point she could have observed all the art work on the walls by slightly altering her position had there not been so many people blocking the view. Someone sat down behind her, and she turned to see that it was Dr. Fletcher. Her skin tingled, and she sought to hide the fluster she felt.

"Are your other paintings half as interesting as these three?" Fletcher asked.

"You'd have to be the judge of that."

Mary plunked down next to Josey. "She's got tons of paintings, and I have gobs of pottery."

Fletcher laughed and took Mary's card out of her pocket to glance at it. "Are you open tomorrow?"

"Nine to five," Mary said.

"Will you both be there?"

Josey smiled to herself. Nothing would keep her away.

Before leaving, the exhibiting artists agreed to go out for lunch the following Saturday after they collected their art. Mary offered to hang some of their artwork on the Pottery and Art Mill walls.

The next day Jewel called the Mill to say the university wanted the *Woman in the Mirror* series as a permanent addition to their art gallery. It would be included in traveling exhibits twice a year. Did Josey have a price in mind?

"What do you think is a fair price?" she asked Jewel.

"Six thousand?"

"Give me a few days."

"Take all week," Jewel said.

She hung up and turned to Mary who had been listening and who now threw her arms around Josey. "I knew it," she said over and over when Josey filled her in on Jewel's side of the conversation.

Josey's heart swelled at Mary's unselfish happiness for her. It caught in her throat so that she almost choked on it. "You are the best friend anyone could have."

Mary drew away. "Don't get carried away. I'm green with jealousy, but your success will get people here to see my stuff."

When the door opened and Lauren Fletcher stepped through it, Mary whispered, "See, see."

Josey felt a rush of joy, followed by less clear emotions. She could have justified refusing a private buyer, but not a gallery looking for the series as a permanent exhibit. The offer spelled success, which she found satisfying, but it also meant exposure. That she was the *Woman in the Mirror* would be ferreted out, she was sure.

The paintings had also brought Fletcher here. She felt the adrenaline racing through her system, telling her that she was attracted to this woman.

XXVI
Annie

Annie poked her head through the door. "She needed me for directions."

"I invited her along for her company as well," Dr. Fletcher said.

Josey and Mary stared at them. Mary recovered first. "The university offered to buy Josey's paintings to add to their permanent collection."

Annie congratulated her aunt, although she suspected she was being kept in the dark. Ashamed because she'd presumed to think her aunt was all right when in fact she had been going through a terrible crisis, she felt foolish and unimportant.

"That's wonderful," Lauren Fletcher exclaimed.

Josey laughed. "Who would have thought?"

Annie watched the grin light up her aunt's eyes, soften her mouth, crinkle around her eyes. She looked almost beautiful in a faded sort of way.

"Mind if I look around?" Dr. Fletcher asked.

"By all means. That's why we have this place. We're like two machines; once set into motion, we can't stop producing."

"It must be marvelous to be so creative," Fletcher murmured.

Annie dropped to the floor to play with Buddy.

"Would you take him outside, Annie? He probably has to tinkle," Josey said.

"Trying to get rid of me?" she asked, standing up.

"It's a pretty day. Thought you might like to enjoy it."

"John Lovelace is going to stop in to see me." She knew he was going to be home on the weekend and had called that morning.

"I'll send him on."

John pulled into the parking lot as she started off the porch. She took the steps two at a time and jumped into his arms, surprised at how glad she was to see him. Now that Molly was spending so much time with Jake, she felt she hadn't a friend in the world. Certainly no one she could confide in, not that she would ever talk about Molly with John.

"Whoa," he said, wrapping wiry arms around her and falling back a few steps to catch his balance. "I missed you too, girl."

Buddy jumped around them, barking excitedly.

Exchanging news, they walked across the dam and started around the pond. John reached for her hand and held it. The sun played hide and seek behind puffy clouds in a pale blue sky. The wind out of the west skittered across the water, ruffling it into wavelets.

"How's your love life?" Annie asked.

"I'm too busy for a love life." John's mouth twisted. "She dumped me."

"I'm sorry," she murmured, leaning over to pick up a flat stone to skip. It plopped a couple of times before sinking.

"Watch this," he told her, bouncing one across the waves. "That's how to do it."

Buddy splashed a few feet into the water after the stone, looking puzzled at its disappearance.

"Silly dog." She laughed, so pleased to be here. They walked on, scuffling through the sand as Buddy raced ahead.

John took her hand again. "How's Molly?"

"She's going with the campus hotshot. Nice guy, though."

"I thought she was going with you."

Her heart faltered for a moment. "What do you mean going with me?"

"I thought you were a, you know, couple. Sort of." He stole a glance at her. "Hey, I don't care who likes who. Or is it whom?"

"Well, I think she's going to dump me, too." Now her heart galloped in angst. What if he spread the news? She'd never be able to come back here.

He put an arm around her and pulled her close. "Sorry, Annie."

She drew a deep breath, fighting tears. "You won't tell anyone, will you?"

"If they torture me, I will." He tightened his grip on her shoulders, then let his arm fall and took her hand again. "Too bad, though, you'd make me a terrific girlfriend."

"I am your girlfriend."

"Yeah, but not the kissy type."

"On the cheek."

"How'd you get here anyway?" he asked.

"With the professor whose class I'm auditing." She told him about Dr. Fletcher.

"You're never going back to Madison, are you? Did you call about your suspension?"

"Nope." How foolish she must look, she thought, chasing after Molly.

The drive home in Fletcher's Audi station wagon passed in relative silence. Fletcher asked a few questions about her aunt, a few more about how Annie was getting along with the short stories, after which followed a long space of silence.

The lack of conversation didn't appear to bother Fletcher. She seemed absorbed in listening to an opera on public radio, while Annie searched her mind for something to talk about. Personal questions weren't an option, and she felt too shallow to discuss much else.

Fletcher glanced at the book in Annie's lap. "You always have a book with you. When did you become such a reader?"

"I don't remember." But the more time Molly spent with Jake, the more time Annie shut them out with a book, just as she had her stepfather, excising him from conscious thought.

"You said in order to write you have to read."

Fletcher smiled. "Voraciously, although I doubt if I've had that kind of influence on any student. Either you love to read or you don't." She spared a glance from the road for Annie. "Is your aunt a reader, too?"

"Yes, and my mother and my sisters. We used to pass books around when I lived at home. I stayed with my aunt this past summer."

"Did you?"

"I couldn't go home after I was suspended." She felt Fletcher's eyes on her but when she looked at her, the professor's gaze was on the road.

"Why was that?"

"My stepfather wouldn't let me. So I went to my aunt's and painted her house."

"That was good of you," she said.

"It's a big old farmhouse, but I figured I paid for my keep."

"Can you go never go home again?"

"I don't want to." She looked out the window. They had left the sandy hills. She had questions to ask Fletcher but thought they would be impertinent and probably unwelcome. Finally, she said, "I read your books of short stories. Jake Boyer lent them to me."

"And?"

"I liked the characters even though I don't really know anyone like them. They were survivors." It was something her mother had said once about some woman who was hospitalized after a beating by her ex-husband.

Fletcher flashed a smile at her. "I grew up with women like the ones in my stories. They have their own brand of respectability."

Now a whole bunch of questions came to her. "Yeah?"

"Yeah. My grandma, my mother, my aunts, my cousins. I was the first to go to college out of the lot. My younger sister followed in my footsteps."

"Where'd you get the money?" The words slipped out and she waited to be chastened.

"Scholarships, grants. You could do the same."

"After getting suspended?"

"Yep. Want to give it a try?"

"I guess." How could she say no, that she liked working part time and auditing Fletcher's class, that she didn't want to take all the classes required for graduation. "I want to audit your writing seminar next semester."

"That's a given. Grants and scholarships take a while."

Fletcher dropped her off at the restaurant. Music flowed from the speakers, and conversation hummed from the mostly full tables. The other waitress, Ginny, threw her a harried look, and Annie hurried to the kitchen to set her backpack in a corner.

The cook and owner looked up at her, a cigarette hanging from his lips. She suspected smoking while cooking for the public was illegal, but she liked him too well to ever say anything. "Grab your apron, honey. Ginny's going nuts."

She glanced at her watch, saw that she was fifteen minutes late, and snatched an order pad. On the floor, she apologized to Ginny and took half the tables.

When they closed, she walked home quickly, hunched against the cool night. No light seeped under the door of her apartment. She saw no need to brace herself.

She thought she was prepared for this, but when Molly and Jake peered over the covers at her, she realized nothing could have made her ready to see them in the sack together. The bedside lamp gave off enough light to illuminate their startled faces.

Annie stared only long enough for the scene to sink in. Knowing that now there could be no denial, she failed to find words to fight through the pain gripping her chest and jumbling her thoughts.

First to speak, Molly said, "I'm sorry, Annie."

"Me, too," Jake added. "We must have fallen asleep."

She backed out of the door. "I'll be back in fifteen minutes." Looking at her watch without really seeing it, she clattered down the stairs and out into the cloudy night.

Her breath puffed little clouds as she stuffed her hands into her pockets and walked toward the campus. She'd go inside to the Commons and read. At least, it would be warm there.

Buying a Pepsi from the machine, she sat in a chair and stared. What she saw was not the space in front of her but Jake and Molly's alarmed faces, Molly's bare shoulders and Jake's hairy chest. Jake had said they'd fallen asleep in a mildly apologetic tone, making her think he didn't know what Molly meant to her. Breathing hurt, as if she'd been punched in the stomach.

She recalled what her aunt had said after she'd caught her in bed with Molly. That it was so sweet while it lasted, but hurt like hell when it was over. She could call Josey from the pay phone. Her aunt had said any time Annie wanted to talk, she was ready to listen. She had a terrible feeling, though, that Josey was the subject for the *Woman in the Mirror*. If Josey couldn't confide in her, then neither could she place her trust in Josey. She realized this was silly, that the years between them would keep Josey from thinking of her niece as a confidante.

She briefly considered sharing Molly with Jake. The thought that she'd probably already been doing so made her angry. Enough so that she realized sharing Molly would tear her apart. Besides, she wasn't sure Molly wanted to be shared.

She went to the pay phone, got as far as lifting the receiver, putting change in the slot, and listening to the ringing, then hung up before Josey could answer. How could she whine to someone who so bravely hid her problems?

When she returned to the apartment, Molly and Jake were gone. There were still traces of Molly lying around, though. Some of her clothes hung on the rack that served as a closet, some lay in the drawer of the battered dresser. Annie found Molly's toothbrush snuggled up to her own in the cup on the same dresser. There was a note on the table.

I'll be over tomorrow morning after my eleven o'clock class. I am sorry, Annie. Molly.

She wouldn't be around when Molly arrived. She'd leave a note for her. Taking three ibuprofen, as if they could ease the ache in her chest, she sat at the table to write something for Tuesday's class but instead found herself composing a brief note.

Molly. I think it's best if we don't see each other. Take your things and leave the key on the table. Annie.

Unable to concentrate on Fletcher's assignment, a character sketch within a descriptive scene, she made a stab at reading and ended up pacing. Around midnight she rolled up in a blanket, having ripped the only sheets off the bed, and tried to sleep. At four in the morning, when she was still awake, she realized that not only was this the worst night of her life, it was the longest.

She finally fell into an exhausted sleep from which Molly wakened her. Annie's eyes ached and she cleared the sleep out of the corners, momentarily forgetting the scene she'd walked in on the previous night.

"Hi." Molly, her eyes shot through with red, stood beside the bed. "I didn't sleep much last night."

Annie pointed at the table. "There's a note for you there." She glanced at her watch and saw that Molly had come early.

"Okay," Molly said with a shrug. "I'll move out." She began gathering her things.

Annie forced herself to say nothing, knowing that if she opened her mouth, she'd ask Molly to stay. She knew she couldn't risk finding Molly in bed with Jake again.

Molly found a bag and stuffed her clothes and toothbrush into it. She carried it toward the door, then turned as if to say something.

"Leave the key," Annie said around a sob.

"I could stay a while." Molly looked her in the eyes.

"No."

"I'm not a lesbian."

A surge of anger came to her rescue. "You'd better go then, because I am."

XXVII
Josey

Josey looked up from the book she was reading at the counter as Roy came into the shop Monday morning.

"Hi, Josey," he said. "I wanted to tell you and my ex-wife I'm going west. I've got a bid on the business and an offer on the house."

"When?" she asked, taken by surprise. How had he kept this a secret in such a small town?

"When the money's in my pocket, I'll start driving."

Mary leaned on the doorframe between the studio and shop. She glowed these days, Josey thought—her skin, her eyes luminous. Roy's news brought on a frown. "Why?" she asked, although she had to know.

Josey knew. He'd lost both Mary and Tom.

"Don't go," Mary said impulsively before he could answer.

"The deed is done," he replied. "Josey." He gave her a hug. "It's mostly been a pleasure. I'll send a postcard when I land."

"You haven't left yet," she pointed out.

"Soon," he said, striding over to Mary and kissing her on the cheek.

Mary's eyes filled up and spilled over. Roy smiled. "I'll see you before I leave. I just wanted to prepare you. Got to go now." He waved a big hand on his way out.

Mary took a few steps as if to stop him. She looked stunned.

"Let him go, Mary. There's nothing here for him anymore." She put an arm around her friend, thinking it was better to be the one leaving than the one left. "Go back to work. Concentrate on Mac." At least, Mary had someone to take Roy's place.

The winter ahead looked long and bleak. Annie was gone; Ellen would leave for La Crosse in January; Mary was caught up in her love affair with Mac; now Roy was going away. She leaned on the counter, staring at the door as if willing someone to come through it. Someone like Lauren Fletcher would be nice, she thought, forcing herself not to dwell on how alone she felt.

She was healing nicely from the surgery. The skin stretcher was in place behind the chest muscle, a swelling behind the muscle, and soon Dr. Lieberman would start filling it with a solution. Because she'd never expected it to happen to her, she'd never given thought to how she'd feel after losing a breast: naked, embarrassed, even freakish. There would always be a scar to mark the mastectomy and one on the other breast if she had the mastopexy to achieve symmetry. When completed, though, she thought she'd achieve a semblance of normality.

Her thoughts strayed again to Lauren Fletcher, who had lingered for a long time in the gallery Sunday. She bought one of Josey's favorite paintings, a watercolor of cedar waxwings in a dead tree. Whenever Josey looked at it, she heard the birds' high-pitched keening in her head. Fletcher had also bought one of Mary's large bowls.

Put out when Mary offered to show Lauren the studio, leaving Josey to wait on a string of unexpected customers, she'd longed to throw everyone out so that she could join them. Straining to hear their conversation, she'd been unable to make out the words.

When the door opened again, Josey felt a foolish surge of hope that Lauren Fletcher would be the one to walk through it. Instead, it was Shelley.

"Aren't you working today?" she asked.

"Cindy Protheroe's filling for me." The police chief's wife. "She used to wait tables before she married Bernie."

"What's up?"

"I heard Roy was leaving town."

"So he says."

"Now that Tom's home every night, I almost wish he wasn't. He's so crabby."

He's going to get a lot crabbier, Josey thought, once he isn't getting any sex. Such melodrama in a small town, a village really.

"I'm thinking I'm gonna tell him to leave. He can live in the maintenance garage. There's a bed and a microwave," Shelley said. "Is Mary here?"

Josey felt only relief to let the onus of advice and comfort fall on Mary. She called for her, and Mary came out of the back room, wiping her hands on a towel.

"I don't know what to tell the boys if I tell Tom to leave." Shelley snatched a couple of tissues from the box on the counter and wiped her eyes.

Josey pictured Tom's sons coming after Roy with their guns. "Don't tell them your suspicions. Who knows what they would do."

"Maybe they'd shoot the bastards," Shelley said with a small, bitter smile.

"And they'd deserve it, but then your boys would go to jail," Mary pointed out.

"There's no justice, is there?" Shelley sighed. "I won't tell anyone. All these years we've been together and it ends up like this. Who would have thought?"

Josey was as surprised as anyone.

"I think I'll go tell him now," Shelley said, squaring her shoulders.

"Want me to come along for moral support?" Mary asked.

"Thanks, but no. I have to do this alone."

Late Thursday afternoon Mary answered the phone, exchanged a few words, and called Josey from the studio.

"For you," Mary said, arching one eyebrow and cocking her head.

"Yes?" Josey spoke into the phone.

"Hi. It's Lauren Fletcher."

Josey experienced a moment of pure elation. "Hi. What can I do for you?"

"You can have dinner with me Saturday evening. You're going to be in town anyway, aren't you?"

Her heart leaped into high gear. She stifled the joy, telling herself that Lauren probably was having a bunch of people over.

"I am and I'd love to have dinner. Tell me what time and how to get there and what to wear." Then she felt foolish about the "what to wear," but she didn't want to be under- or overdressed.

"Whatever you wear will be fine, since it'll be just the two of us."

The "two of us" rang in her mind. She didn't question her excitement until after she hung up and noticed Mary's expression. Her hands were slick with sweat and she wiped them on her jeans.

"Why are you looking at me like that?"

"I think there's something hatching here. Have you and Ellen given up on each other?"

"Ellen's moving to La Crosse. I'm staying here. You know that."

"There are long-distance relationships that work."

"We're good friends, that's all. I wish it had turned into more. It would be easier."

Mary looked a little disappointed. "I like Ellen. She's got class."

"I agree, but so does Lauren Fletcher." She tried to make Mary understand. "You know how you feel about Mac, how you can't wait to be alone? There's a mutual passion between you two that Ellen and I don't have and never will."

206

"How can you have passion for Lauren Fletcher? You don't know her."

Josey laughed. "We're having dinner together Saturday evening. I'll get to know her."

Saturday morning, Josey took Buddy to the Mill. "He's got that abandonment complex, you know." She reached down to pat the dog, who somehow seemed to know she was leaving without him. "I'll be back, Buddy." She knew he would watch the door, waiting for her to return.

"He'll forget you as soon as you're gone. Trust me," Mary said. "I'll take him home with me tonight." She pushed Josey toward the door. "Go on. Have a good time."

She gave Mary a hug and the dog another pat, then stepped outside into the cold wind.

She hardly remembered the drive into town. Parking behind the gallery, she went inside. After exchanging greetings with the other artists, she phoned her niece.

"Annie? I want to see you before you go to work, but I'm having lunch with the other artists here. Can I meet you at your apartment after one-thirty?"

"If you don't have time, it's okay," the girl said in a quiet voice.

"I'll make time. Okay?"

"Okay. I'll be here."

"We're going down the street to Victoria's," Jewel said when Josey hung up. "I have the check here for your paintings. They were picked up earlier. You must go over to see them."

"Think they'll be hung already?" When she took the check, she felt the thrill of being acknowledged. But she wasn't fooled. Marketing was difficult and time consuming and costly. It wasn't her thing either. This success was a step, but it wouldn't make her famous nor sought after.

Lunch at Victoria's was noisy and heartening. Her fellow

exhibitors raised a toast to her, and she to them. Their talk was of art and technique and selling. When they left, they exchanged e-mail addresses, promising to keep in touch.

Driving to Annie's apartment, Josey belatedly picked up on the tone of her niece's voice on the phone. She guessed Molly had given Annie the shaft, but she could think of nothing to say that would ease the pain.

Annie was seated on the top step of the apartment house, her chin in her hands, dressed in a large sweater and jeans. She got up when Josey parked in the small lot next to the building.

"Cold out here," Josey said. She'd seldom shown Annie physical affection. Giving the girl an awkward hug, she felt warmth spread through her when Annie returned the embrace. They stood like that for a few moments before separating.

Josey laughed a little, embarrassed by the emotion. "Let's go where we can talk."

"Upstairs." Annie led the way.

Inside, the faded papered walls gave off a mildewy odor. It had once been a lovely home. The hallway and staircase were wide, the woodwork a dark oak. Josey would have bet that the floors under the brown, worn carpeting were also oak. The doors to all the apartments were closed.

Josey followed Annie into the large room. The upright registers were festooned with drying underwear and socks, the table littered with papers, books lay on the bed and floor. Looking around, Josey saw no evidence of someone else, but then Molly's belongings would resemble her niece's. So when she said, "I've lost more than one lover and so will you," she was flying blind.

"How did you know?" Annie asked, her eyes tired and sad. She looked as if she'd lost weight. Her face crumpled, and Josey saw the little girl she had once been.

"I guessed." She continued gently, "Look, I know how it hurts. You think you're going to die and almost wish you would, but you don't. It takes time to heal. If you think it'll help, call me when it gets too hard and I'll come and take you home for a while. Sometimes it helps just to have people around."

Later they walked to the art gallery, where Josey's paintings hung on the wall. Standing in front of them, Josey felt as if she'd lost something valuable.

"You should be proud, Josey. I am," her niece said. "I'm going to tell everyone that you're my aunt."

"Don't bother."

"You belong to the world now," Annie said, and Josey laughed.

"You are dramatic."

The girl looked at her earnestly. "This happened to you, didn't it?"

Josey chewed on her lower lip, thinking it hadn't been fair to keep it from Annie. "Yes."

"I won't tell."

"Thanks." Searching Annie's eyes, Josey realized that, although she still didn't want to talk about it, she no longer particularly cared who else knew.

She dropped Annie off at the restaurant and searched out Lauren Fletcher's home. It was a neat, little brick house set on a back street behind the campus. Lauren flew out the front door as she backed out of the driveway.

"I was just finding the place before dark set in," Josey said, rolling down her window.

"Park in the driveway and come on in. I'm glad you're early."

She did as Lauren bid, grabbing the bottle of wine she purchased for the occasion and slipping through the door Fletcher held open for her into a small foyer. One side opened to a dining room, the other to the living room, straight ahead a stairway climbed to the second floor, and alongside it a hall lead to a bathroom under the stairs and the kitchen beyond.

"Thanks," Lauren said, taking the wine and reading the label.

"What a lovely place." Josey peered into the living room that spanned the house front to back. Light flowed through paneled windows. Wood floors were accented with brightly colored, braided rugs. A fire burned in the fireplace, and Josey's painting of the cedar waxwings hung over the mantel.

"Looks nice there, doesn't it?" Lauren said.

"I hope you didn't feel you had to put it in that spot just for me."

"Nope. I've been looking for something to hang there for a long time. Care to sit down?"

Josey settled on the leather couch and laughed when she noticed Mary's bowl on the coffee table. "Mary would be pleased." There were nuts in the bowl. "She likes her pottery to be useful."

A smile lit Lauren's face and eyes. "I am so glad you could come. Have you seen your paintings at the university?"

"Yes. Annie and I walked over to the gallery."

"How did you feel?"

Josey looked away. "Like I'd lost a part of me."

"You did, didn't you?" Lauren asked.

"Yes, I did." She met Lauren's eyes. "It's not something I like to talk about."

"It happened to me. It seems like there's an epidemic of breast cancer out there."

Taken aback, she said, "And what did you do for therapy? Write a book?"

Lauren's smile turned rueful, but her eyes never left Josey's face. "Yes, but about something else. I admired your courage."

Startled, Josey met the unflinching gaze. "It wasn't courage, that's for sure. Mary had to push me into exhibiting the series."

"Would you like a drink or a glass of wine?" Lauren asked.

"Whatever you're having."

She followed Lauren into the kitchen, a small, functional room with ceramic tile floors, glass fronted oak cabinets, and windows that looked out the back and side of the house. A door led to an outside patio, and an archway opened into the dining room.

"I'm having a glass of Merlot, but I have vodka, gin, and whiskey on hand."

"Merlot is fine. I have to drive home tonight."

"I do have two extra bedrooms, unless there's some compelling reason you have to go home." A faint flush colored Lauren's cheeks, and she kept her eyes on the glass as she handed it to Josey.

Returning to the living room, Lauren threw a log on the fire. Sparks flew and she closed the screens but not the glass doors. Josey sipped the wine and stared at the flames.

Lauren sat down next to her. "Tell me about your house."

Josey laughed, embarrassed at the thought of Lauren seeing where she lived. She shook her head. "It's just a big old farmhouse."

After dinner, they again sat on the couch in the living room. "How did it get so late?" Josey had arrived before four. It was now nine.

"Why don't you stay the night?" Lauren said.

Rain fell outside, the roads would be black, and she'd had several glasses of wine. "I'd have to leave first thing in the morning."

"Good. I'd worry about you driving home tonight."

"I'd worry about me, too," Josey said, realizing that she was slightly impaired by the wine.

Lauren moved closer. She took Josey's hand. Josey looked at her mouth, the lips full and softly crumpled, and leaned forward to kiss her. Her heartbeat filled her ears. She pulled back in alarm. "The wine did that. I'm sorry. I really should go home."

"Don't. Please. It's dark and cold and wet out there. This is enough for tonight. I'm not one to jump into things either."

Later, Lauren showed her to a bedroom across the hall from her own. She lay in bed, listening to the rain tapping against the windows, thinking about the desire Lauren stirred in her. Where it came from, and why Lauren and not Ellen aroused it, was beyond her understanding. She welcomed it, though, knowing that desire like this might not come again in her lifetime. She would not turn away from Lauren willingly.

March

XXVIII

The horse fair brought Josey more business on the first day than she expected for the entire coming year. She had agreed to paint Monty Junior and Snipper's foal by Monty Senior. When so many others lined up for her services, she worried that she'd started a fad and might never get back to serious work.

She drove to Appleton on Friday, spent the night with Lauren, and brought Annie to the horse fair with her the next day. Her niece and John and Candy planned to meet there.

Annie looked paler and thinner than Josey had ever seen her. "Don't you eat, Annie?" she asked as they drove south on Highway 41 to the Oshkosh fairgrounds.

"I'm not very hungry. There's no one to eat with."

"I know what that's like," Josey agreed. Who wanted to cook for one? It seemed like a waste of time. "Get some frozen meals."

"My freezer doesn't work."

"What are you eating?"

"Peanut butter sandwiches and bananas and carrots. I figure I'm hitting all the food categories." A smile.

"Are you coming back to Clover for the summer? We could use you at the Mill." Especially now that she had contracts for all these equine portraits.

"I'd like working for you and Mary," Annie said. "What about Dr. Fletcher? Is she spending the summer with you?"

Josey cleared her throat. She wasn't really comfortable discussing her love life with Annie, especially since Lauren had not only helped Annie apply for a scholarship but vouched for her, too. "Some of the time. She wants to get away to finish a book she's working on. She thinks the old homestead is ideal."

Josey had been embarrassed when she'd first taken Lauren to the house. It had been a snowy winter day, and they'd lit the fireplace in the living room and huddled together on the couch, drinking wine and talking.

"This is a great getaway," Lauren had said, looking around the dimly lit room Josey seldom used.

Everything looked ancient to Josey, the walls in need of paint, the threadbare carpeting, the dusty furniture. "I've let the place go," she admitted sadly.

"It's great just the way it is. Comfortable but not pretentious."

Josey hadn't believed she meant it. Rundown was more like it. She'd vowed to paint the walls and tear the carpeting up first chance she got, but with running back and forth to see Lauren, she'd never found the time.

She said to Annie, "I need you to help me fix up the inside of the house, too. I've got all these horse portraits to do." She thought how different her financial prospects appeared this year as opposed to last. She'd paid her medical bills with the proceeds from the sale of *Woman in the Mirror*.

"I can do that," Annie said, "and work at the Mill."

✦

Josey returned to Appleton alone, and Annie left earlier with Candy and John, who were now an item. She drove to Lauren's house, let herself in the front door, and walked down the hall to the kitchen. Lauren looked up with a welcoming smile.

"How was the horse fair?"

"Too good. I'll never get all these horses on canvas. And if I do, I'll never have time to do any other work."

"Wonderful news today." Lauren tossed a letter toward Josey. "Do you know where Annie is?"

Annie had her scholarship. She'd still have to pay for housing and books, but her tuition would be covered. "We could call her at work, but why don't you tell her in person?"

"I will. After the next seminar."

"I can't begin to tell you how much I appreciate what you've done for her," Josey said.

"I would have done it for anyone who shows talent. She just happens to be your niece. I think we should be a little discreet about that, though. Don't you?"

"Definitely, but I'm not giving you up, even if I have to pay her tuition." As if she had that kind of money to spare. "I bought her a computer."

"What about her mom?"

"She'll pay for most of the room and board."

"Want to make love?" Lauren never skirted issues. If she wanted something, she asked.

They climbed the stairs to Lauren's bedroom—a large, well lit space with double-hung windows, scattered rugs on bare wood floors, a double bed, dresser, bedside tables, books everywhere. It spoke of comfort rather than style.

It was difficult for Josey to believe her good fortune. She felt only a little sadness when she thought of Ellen gone to La Crosse. They had parted as friends and exchanged e-mails.

Josey had never had a lover who wanted her so much. In the

months since she and Lauren began making love, Lauren's insistent passion never failed to arouse her own.

"Come on, take those horsey clothes off." Lauren started unbuttoning Josey's flannel shirt.

They were in too much of a hurry to bother with completely undressing. Lying in a tangle of limbs, panting in the aftermath, Josey knew slower, more satisfying lovemaking would follow.

Josey felt completed for the first time in her life. Never was she lonely anymore, knowing that Lauren was at most a phone call away. She looked forward to the summer months, which Lauren would spend with her and Annie, and put off thoughts of winter when she and Buddy would be rattling around the big farmhouse, alone except on weekends.

She'd toyed with thoughts of moving in with Lauren during the winter months and using the farmhouse as a seasonal home. Summer was the only time they needed more than one person at the Mill. Mary would understand. But she wasn't ready to leave Clover even to go as far as Appleton. For now, she'd let things remain as they were. Something would work out.

May

XXIX

Annie had her clothes packed when Josey arrived with the Escort. Together they carried her few belongings out to the station wagon. When they were done, she stood in the sparsely furnished room and turned a slow circle before closing the door.

It ended a chapter of her life. Next fall she'd return as a student, although she wouldn't room in this house. She'd take an apartment elsewhere rather than live in a dorm. Her mother, thrilled about the scholarship, had promised to pay the housing as long as Annie paid for books. Josey had insisted on buying her a computer, saying she couldn't write without one. It would be like trying to paint without supplies.

She had a lot to be grateful for, but no one had turned up to take Molly's place in her heart and her bed. Whenever she saw Jake in the creative writing seminar, she was hardly able to be civil to him. He'd told her he'd proposed to Molly, that they were to be married after graduation.

She passed this information on to Josey as they drove out of the city, the dog perched on Annie's lap, his nose poked out the open window.

"What a mistake. She doesn't even know who she is." Josey shook her head.

"I don't know who I am either." Annie looked out the window at the newly leafed trees. A year had passed since she'd been suspended at Madison. She would never have thought then that she'd be where she was now.

"You're a writer. You got a scholarship because of it." Josey looked pleased.

"Dr. Fletcher got me the scholarship."

"She wouldn't have helped you get it if she hadn't thought you deserved it."

Annie wondered. Perhaps Fletcher's feelings for her aunt had played a part in it, but Fletcher had mentioned a scholarship before she'd met Josey. Who would have guessed that her aunt and her professor would become lovers? If it could happen to them, it could happen to her again.

She wasn't sure she could live through another Molly experience right now. She'd hang out with John and Candy and Rog and maybe be around when Cass found out Molly was engaged to Jake. If her aunt and Lauren Fletcher were examples, there was passion after forty. She had years to look for someone before she reached forty. The looking, she thought, might be more fun than the finding.

They turned off Highway 10 and the road began to rise. Trees edged the berm, flowers nodded in the ditches as they headed into the sandy hills toward the many lakes, the meandering trout streams, and Josey's old farmhouse. Annie smiled in anticipation. To her, it all felt like coming home.

About the Author

Jackie Calhoun lives with her partner in northeast Wisconsin. She is the author of *Outside the Flock*, *Tamarack Creek*, and *Off Season*, published by Bella Books; ten romance novels by Naiad Press; and *Crossing the Center Line*, printed by Windstorm Creative Ltd. Calhoun divides her time between her home on the Fox River, her family's lake cottage in central Wisconsin, and her partner's lake cabin in northern Wisconsin. She writes of a Wisconsin not represented by dairy cattle and/or the Packers, but by its many lakes, trout streams, rivers, and forests.

CAUGHT IN THE NET by Jessica Thomas. 188 pp. A wickedly observant story of mystery, danger, and love in Provincetown. ISBN 1-931513-54-6 $12.95

DREAMS FOUND by Lyn Denison. Australian Riley embarks on a journey to meet her birth mother . . . and gains not just a family, but the love of her life. ISBN 1-931513-58-9 $12.95

A MOMENT'S INDISCRETION by Peggy J. Herring. 154 pp. Jackie is torn between her better judgment and the overwhelming attraction she feels for Valerie. ISBN 1-931513-59-7 $12.95

IN EVERY PORT by Karin Kallmaker. 224 pp. Jessica's sexy, adventuresome travels. ISBN 1-931513-36-8 $12.95

TOUCHWOOD by Karin Kallmaker. 240 pp. Loving May/December romance. ISBN 1-931513-37-6 $12.95

WATERMARK by Karin Kallmaker. 248 pp. One burning question . . . how to lead her back to love? ISBN 1-931513-38-4 $12.95

EMBRACE IN MOTION by Karin Kallmaker. 240 pp. A whirlwind love affair. ISBN 1-931513-39-2 $12.95

ONE DEGREE OF SEPARATION by Karin Kallmaker. 232 pp. Can an Iowa City librarian find love and passion when a California girl surfs into the close-knit dyke capital of the Midwest? ISBN 1-931513-30-9 $12.95

CRY HAVOC A Detective Franco Mystery by Baxter Clare. 240 pp. A dead hustler with a headless rooster in his lap sends Lt. L.A. Franco headfirst against Mother Love. ISBN 1-931513931-7 $12.95

DISTANT THUNDER by Peggy J. Herring. 294 pp. Bankrobbing drifter Cordy awakens strange new feelings in Leo in this romantic tale set in the Old West. ISBN 1-931513-28-7 $12.95

COP OUT by Claire McNab. 216 pp. 4th Detective Inspector Carol Ashton Mystery. ISBN 1-931513-29-5 $12.95

BLOOD LINK by Claire McNab. 159 pp. 15th Detective Inspector Carol Ashton Mystery. Is Carol unwittingly playing into a deadly plan? ISBN 1-931513-27-9 $12.95

TALK OF THE TOWN by Saxon Bennett. 239 pp. With enough beer, barbecue and B.S., anything is possible! ISBN 1-931513-18-X $12.95

MAYBE NEXT TIME by Karin Kallmaker. 256 pp. Sabrina Starling has it all: fame, money, women—and pain. Nothing hurts like the one that got away. ISBN 1-931513-26-0 $12.95

WHEN GOOD GIRLS GO BAD: A Motor City Thriller by Therese Szymanski. 230 pp. Brett, Randi, and Allie join forces to stop a serial killer. ISBN 1-931513-11-2 $12.95

A DAY TOO LONG: A Helen Black Mystery by Pat Welch. 328 pp. This time Helen's fate is in her own hands. ISBN 1-931513-22-8 $12.95

THE RED LINE OF YARMALD by Diana Rivers. 256 pp. The Hadra's only hope lies in a magical red line . . . climactic sequel to *Clouds of War*. ISBN 1-931513-23-6 $12.95

OUTSIDE THE FLOCK by Jackie Calhoun. 224 pp. Jo embraces her new love and life. ISBN 1-931513-13-9 $12.95

LEGACY OF LOVE by Marianne K. Martin. 224 pp. Read the whole Sage Bristo story.
ISBN 1-931513-15-5 $12.95

STREET RULES: A Detective Franco Mystery by Baxter Clare. 304 pp. Gritty, fast-paced mystery with compelling Detective L.A. Franco   ISBN 1-931513-14-7 $12.95

RECOGNITION FACTOR: 4th Denise Cleever Thriller by Claire McNab. 176 pp. Denise Cleever tracks a notorious terrorist to America.   ISBN 1-931513-24-4 $12.95

NORA AND LIZ by Nancy Garden. 296 pp. Lesbian romance by the author of *Annie on My Mind*.   ISBN 1931513-20-1 $12.95

MIDAS TOUCH by Frankie J. Jones. 208 pp. Sandra had everything but love.
ISBN 1-931513-21-X $12.95

BEYOND ALL REASON by Peggy J. Herring. 240 pp. A romance hotter than Texas.
ISBN 1-9513-25-2 $12.95

ACCIDENTAL MURDER: 14th Detective Inspector Carol Ashton Mystery by Claire McNab. 208 pp. Carol Ashton tracks an elusive killer.   ISBN 1-931513-16-3 $12.95

SEEDS OF FIRE: Tunnel of Light Trilogy, Book 2 by Karin Kallmaker writing as Laura Adams. 274 pp. Intriguing sequel to *Sleight of Hand*.   ISBN 1-931513-19-8 $12.95

DRIFTING AT THE BOTTOM OF THE WORLD by Auden Bailey. 288 pp. Beautifully written first novel set in Antarctica.   ISBN 1-931513-17-1 $12.95

CLOUDS OF WAR by Diana Rivers. 288 pp. Women unite to defend Zelindar!
ISBN 1-931513-12-0 $12.95

DEATHS OF JOCASTA: 2nd Micky Knight Mystery by J.M. Redmann. 408 pp. Sexy and intriguing Lambda Literary Award-nominated mystery.   ISBN 1-931513-10-4 $12.95

LOVE IN THE BALANCE by Marianne K. Martin. 256 pp. The classic lesbian love story, back in print!   ISBN 1-931513-08-2 $12.95

THE COMFORT OF STRANGERS by Peggy J. Herring. 272 pp. Lela's work was her passion . . . until now.   ISBN 1-931513-09-0 $12.95

CHICKEN by Paula Martinac. 208 pp. Lynn finds that the only thing harder than being in a lesbian relationship is ending one.   ISBN 1-931513-07-4 $11.95

TAMARACK CREEK by Jackie Calhoun. 208 pp. An intriguing story of love and danger.
ISBN 1-931513-06-6 $11.95

DEATH BY THE RIVERSIDE: 1st Micky Knight Mystery by J.M. Redmann. 320 pp. Finally back in print, the book that launched the Lambda Literary Award–winning Micky Knight mystery series.   ISBN 1-931513-05-8 $11.95

EIGHTH DAY: A Cassidy James Mystery by Kate Calloway. 272 pp. In the eighth installment of the Cassidy James mystery series, Cassidy goes undercover at a camp for troubled teens.   ISBN 1-931513-04-X $11.95

MIRRORS by Marianne K. Martin. 208 pp. Jean Carson and Shayna Bradley fight for a future together.   ISBN 1-931513-02-3 $11.95

THE ULTIMATE EXIT STRATEGY: A Virginia Kelly Mystery by Nikki Baker. 240 pp. The long-awaited return of the wickedly observant Virginia Kelly.
ISBN 1-931513-03-1 $11.95